PRAISE for the Wins...

"J.J. Chow has written a great mystery, mixing seniors, video games, and quirky characters together in a perfect blend."
— Trudi LoPreto, Readers' Favorite (5-star review)

"This is a well-written story that intertwines Asian culture and values . . . and very likable and unique characters."
— Christa Reads and Write

"A book that will make you laugh, with fun witty characters and a story line so good you won't want to stop reading it."
— Shelley's Book Case

"Winston Wong, a slacker game developer in the middle of Silicon Valley, is a completely charming rookie sleuth. His modern high-tech world intersects the old, as Winston finds himself embroiled in a suspicious death at a senior home. J.J. Chow adds a fresh, original voice to the mystery genre! I can't wait to read more of Winston's adventures."
— Naomi Hirahara, Edgar Award-winning author of the Mas Arai and Officer Ellie Rush mysteries

"J.J. Chow's *Robot Revenge* is a must-read for cozy mystery fans. In this delightful sequel to *Seniors Sleuth*, we follow Winston Wong as he tracks the killer of a local crime watch captain, only to discover an entire neighborhood of suspects. It's a well-written story of suburban intrigue."
— Janice Peacock, author of the Glass Bead Mystery Series

D1528607

WEDDING WOES

a Winston Wong mystery

J.J. Chow

Cover design by Heena Thombre
Edited by Linda G. Hatton

ALSO BY J.J. CHOW

Seniors Sleuth (Winston Wong Cozy Mystery, Book 1)

Robot Revenge (Winston Wong Cozy Mystery, Book 2)

The 228 Legacy

Dragonfly Dreams

FOR STAN,

Wishing you much joy in matters of the heart.

Family Tree

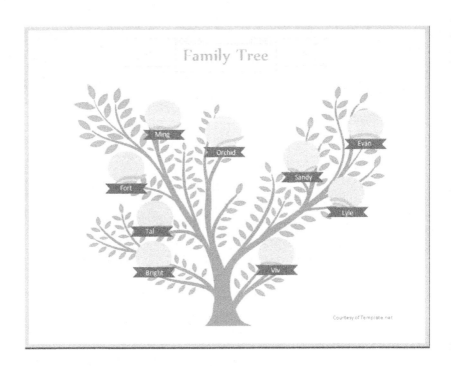

CHAPTER 1

WINSTON LOOKED AT the empty space where the stack of wedding invitations had been. The clutter finally disappeared last month. One week left now until the big date.

Grinning, he recalled every detail of the expensive invites. The front of each ivory envelope bore the name of a friend or relative, done in painstaking calligraphy, thanks to his neighbor Heather on Magnolia Lane. Grateful that Winston had solved the murder of the neighborhood watch captain, she'd donated her artistic skill.

He'd also hired her in an official capacity to plan the wedding dinner. A full traditional ten-course banquet at an exquisite Chinese restaurant in Cupertino. Nothing but the best for his sweet bride-to-be.

Winston and Kristy had finally finished all the preparations after a marathon of planning. Who knew there would be so many choices to make? From floral centerpieces to music to entrees. Thankfully, ever since her youth, Kristy had possessed a solid vision of what she wanted. In fact, she'd shown him the scrapbook of magazine clippings tucked into her hope chest.

Why she hadn't been snapped up earlier remained a mystery to Winston, even with his enormous sleuthing skills. Maybe because she'd been too busy taking care of her younger brothers when their parents died? Or since she'd focused so much dedication to the elderly in her nursing career?

The phone rang, breaking into his thoughts. When he answered the call, he heard a flustered voice saying, "Mr. Wong?"

"That's me."

"I think our intern made a mistake that I just caught."

"Er, who is this?"

The voice introduced herself as staff from the Winchester Mystery House. Winston and Kristy had booked their wedding outside the mansion, on its beautifully paved grounds, figuring their guests would get a kick out of the unique venue.

Winston said, "Yes, we're very much looking forward to having our wedding there."

"Unfortunately, sir, the intern double-booked."

Was this a courtesy call? Winston cleared his throat and used a kind tone. "No matter. Tell the boy we appreciate his gesture, but he doesn't need to send his apologies. He can just kindly explain the mix-up to the other people."

A sigh floated down the line. "Actually, the other party booked first."

"Wait, what? But we have a contract."

"Do you really? Because I can't locate it in our computer system. What we actually have is a scribbled note in our intern's handwriting."

Winston couldn't believe it. He checked for the paperwork in his filing cabinet. Then he consulted his email. "I can't find it. But he definitely told me face-to-face."

"A verbal agreement? I'm afraid, Mr. Wong, we have documentation from a year ago reserving the same date." She took a deep breath, and her voice trembled when she dropped the other groom's name, a Hollywood A-lister. "Not that it matters. We treat everyone the same."

Yeah, right.

She continued speaking. "How about a different day?"

He gritted his teeth. "I can't. We already sent out the invites and everything. People will be flying in. They've bought tickets, booked hotels."

"We're really sorry. To make amends, I can send you a discounted admission for your next visit."

Winston couldn't speak. He slammed his fist against his desk. His wedding venue was cancelled and all he got in return was a coupon?

The woman on the phone took his silence as assent. "I'm glad we settled things. Thank you for your understanding."

She hung up, and Winston stared at his phone. What had just happened? If only he could reboot the whole conversation. He had been the one responsible for the venue. Just the other day, he'd reassured Kristy that things were settled on his end. He shook his head to clear it.

How could he fix this? Turning to his trusty computer, he googled "wedding + Winchester mystery." He found an interesting hit on the screen. It wasn't an old cobweb site, but a recently created webpage. It featured a location with amazing scenery in the expansive backyard of somebody's mansion. It even had its own replica of the house, called the "Mystery Shack."

Winston dialed the number and got a live person right away. Wait a minute. He recognized that voice. "Alex?"

"Winston? Why are you calling the new business line?"

He took a deep breath. "It's about the wedding. I need your help."

"Shoot, Winston. What's a best man for?"

CHAPTER 2

WINSTON DIDN'T HAVE time to check out the Mystery Shack until right before the rehearsal date. Of course, he'd been bogged down with his usual cases: seniors needing to locate misplaced items, lost pets, and even wayward grandchildren. On top of that, he'd been rerouting all the vendors to the new location. He'd had to keep a checklist to make sure he contacted everybody he needed to inform—musicians, florists, caterers, etc.

Kristy had been even more occupied. She'd recently taken on double shifts at Life Circles when a coworker had quit out of the blue. "Burnout," Kristy had said over the phone. (They didn't even have time to enjoy face-to-face conversations anymore.) Plus, she'd tasked herself with calling, emailing, and texting all their attendees to make sure they arrived at the correct wedding venue.

The day before the rehearsal, he and Kristy had wanted to check out the place together. But she'd had to drop out when she discovered her gown didn't fit anymore. All the stress had shaved pounds off, and she needed a refitting done. Though the two of them had already preplanned arrangements based on the virtual tour on Alex's website, Winston promised to take lots of pictures and videos of the space as he explored it in real time.

Winston followed the directions from his GPS and found himself driving down an impossibly long cobblestone path. The forbidding and elegant palace he saw must be Alex's new digs, a far cry from his friend's bachelor pad of a pistachio green townhouse. The place hadn't been purchased on Alex's dime, but off the profits from the scandalous memoir his girlfriend Carmen had penned. Her account of her murdering grandmother had placed her book on the bestsellers' lists and earned a major movie deal.

The new house looked like a real castle, complete with turrets. Winston half expected to find a moat surrounding the front entrance. Instead, without getting blocked by any water barrier, he walked up to the front door. He rang the bell, and Alex opened it right away.

They gave each other a half pat on the back to say hello.

"Fancy place," Winston said, gesturing to the grandeur around him.

"Nah. Too drafty," Alex said. "Costs a fortune to heat the space." But the man was grinning—and Winston also noticed Alex's new tailored clothes.

Winston pointed to his friend's fancy outfit. "Snazzy. Is that lapel monogrammed?"

Alex shrugged. "Carmen likes to customize our clothes."

"No more T-shirts then?"

"Not anymore." Alex glanced over his shoulder, and Winston could hear a vacuum humming in the background. "Sorry, but I can't give you the grand tour right now. The cleaning lady's here."

Alex gestured to a path around the side of the house. "Want to take a look outside now?"

"You mean, at your new business venture, the Mystery Shack?"

"Yes, but let's see the grounds first. They'll be perfect for your outdoor wedding."

Winston looked up at the bright sky, almost blinding in its pure blue. "A beautiful weekend's forecasted, but I keep checking the weather report—five times already today. We don't have a backup indoor venue."

"Don't worry, buddy. The weather's cooperating." Alex ushered Winston along the footpath. "Plus, our backyard is gorgeous. Beats that famous Winchester place any day."

As they walked along, Winston's jaw dropped in admiration. Alex had a veritable forest behind his house. Tall pine trees jostled one another for space. Winston pulled out his camera to snap photos and take videos.

"Get a load of this." Alex motioned for Winston to hurry up.

They emerged into a clearing surrounded by majestic trees. Almost auto*magically*, birds started serenading them with a chorus of cheer. An elegant latticed gazebo stood at the far end.

"Amazing," Winston said. "Kristy will love it."

"Told you." Alex slapped Winston on the back.

Winston had visions of Kristy dressed in white (the actual gown was fuzzy in his mind, though, since she'd forbidden him to see it). He could picture her gazing at him with unquenched longing.

He and Alex discussed the placement of chairs and other logistics. Afterward, Alex said, "Now that you're satisfied, let's move on."

They walked toward a connected path, half-hidden by lush growth. A few yards from the clearing stood a small rickety building.

"The Mystery Shack?" Winston guessed.

"Yup. Let me show you around."

"Er, is it safe?" Winston asked, peering at the unsteady-looking structure.

Alex laughed away Winston's worry. "Whatever. I monitored the making of it myself."

"But you have no construction experience."

"Just you wait and see. It'll be a top tourist destination. People who can't get enough of Carmen's book will be paying big bucks to see a shack dreamed up by a murdering grandmother."

Winston frowned. "Isn't it brand-new?"

"Visitors won't know that."

Winston eyed the building. It did appear ancient and ramshackle, but maybe that was the quality of the materials showing. "And you got a permit to build this, right?"

Alex didn't answer and proceeded to enter the shack. Winston hustled to follow, if only to save Alex from a possible falling beam.

The inside of the building was larger than Winston had imagined. The main room had no furnishings except for a rickety rocking chair and a splintering antique desk. They wound their way through twists and turns to examine the few rooms in the shack—and also one door that led only to a tiny hidey-hole. Each room they passed was crammed with shelves holding weird stuff like faded crime scene tape, rusted handcuffs, and scattered bullet casings. Then they returned to the main room, its most unique feature a small staircase, which stopped in midair.

Winston shuddered. "Creepy."

"What about that mansion you were thinking of having your wedding at? Sarah Winchester used to hold séances to figure out how to build *her* home. Now that's weird."

As soon as they exited the shack, Winston gulped in the clean air. He'd felt trapped inside. "Why'd you build that thing anyway?"

Alex clucked his tongue at Winston. "We gotta capitalize on Carmen's memoir. The shack's a great tie-in to show folks the relics of her murdering grandma."

"Did she own any of those things?"

"Nope. Got everything off eBay."

Winston cleared his throat. "The shack's so much smaller than the real Winchester Mystery House, though. Will people actually visit it?"

"Come on, man. Who wants to pay full price when they can get a deal? Same experience at half the price."

"I don't know," Winston said. "Maybe you should stick to something you know, doing voice recordings for video games."

"I'll have you know that I already have a tour group booked for tomorrow afternoon."

Winston blinked at his friend. "But that's when we have the wedding rehearsal scheduled for."

"Hakuna matata, buddy." Alex gave him a hang-loose sign. "I bet you never even notice they're here."

CHAPTER 3

THE SKY HELD floating fluffy clouds, and the trees above him poured out their shade. However, standing in front of the latticed gazebo, Winston felt a drop of sweat inch down his neck. He wiped it away and looked over the crowd. Okay, so there were only four people in the audience. He spied Alex's girlfriend, Carmen, along with his brother-in-law Gary. To their right sat two seniors, Pete and Jazzman, both ex-residents of the Sweet Breeze facility where he'd cracked his first case.

He glanced to his left at his best man. At least, Alex seemed composed, mouthing "Chin up" at him.

His groomsmen, Kristy's brothers, both gave him encouraging head nods. The celebrant—a squat bald man, and one of Winston's regular senior clients (always losing his cat)—patted Winston's shoulder. "Breathe," he said.

Winston inhaled, exhaled. Then he heard the sound system click on. Strains of classical music floated in the air, and he saw Anastasia gliding toward him. Like she had before at the Sweet Breeze senior home, the regal old lady wore voluminous layers. The fabric shimmered in light purple, in honor of the wedding colors. Weighed down by an inordinate amount of jewelry (maybe one piece for each year of her long life?), she walked with tiny but firm steps toward Winston. She passed by and stood on the opposite end of the gazebo. When she winked at him, he felt a calming sense of relief.

Next, his sister, Marcy, came trotting across the clearing, heading toward Anastasia. She locked eyes with Winston, gave him a thumbs-up, and whispered, "Way to go, *sai lo*." Even though he'd passed the forty-year mark, she still called him "little brother" with affection on special occasions.

Finally, "Chances Are" pumped out of the speakers. Their song. He watched as Kristy waltzed toward him, a smile on her lush lips. She wore a simple green sheath dress that brought out her coffee-colored eyes. In this idyllic nature setting, Winston could almost believe her to be a beautiful tree sprite appearing from the nearby forest.

My bride, Winston thought. (Well, almost.) The power of the word struck him with full force. He couldn't concentrate on the rehearsal after that, the precise outlining of the proceedings. Only when the time came for the vow rehearsal did he return to reality.

A sudden fear gripped him. Where had he placed those rings? Made from titanium, the bands symbolized their enduring relationship. Winston peeked in his shirt pocket and patted down his pants. Nothing.

Sweat started buffeting him like relentless ocean waves. Wetness dampened the back of his shirt. The anxiety-induced storm he'd unleashed even drenched his socks.

A hand gripped his shoulder. Alex leaned over, and Winston smelled his buddy's Doritos breath. "You okay, man?"

"The rings," Winston whispered, glancing with alarm at his lovely fiancée standing a few feet away, still smiling with ignorance.

"Yesterday you told me to keep them," Alex said. "So you wouldn't forget."

"Oh, yeah." Winston had had enough to worry about without carrying the rings. Besides, that was a best man's duty, right? "Great, where are they?"

"Er, somewhere in the house. I'll find them before tomorrow, I swear. And in the meantime, I did you one better." Alex nudged Winston in the ribs with his elbow before pulling out two Ring Pops.

Winston stifled a groan.

"Hey, it's even better this way. The real ones are probably on my dresser, safe and sound. Use these for practice."

Winston took the candy. To Kristy's credit, she didn't bat an eyelash at the substitution. They continued on with the exchange of vows. Winston and Kristy had chosen to follow the standard repetition of stock phrases. He again stared into her enchanting eyes, the variations of brown drawing him in and centering him. Everything would be all right with Kristy by his side.

And that's when the ragtag bunch stumbled in. A group of nine Asians, ranging in age, came forward.

"*Ni doh?*" the elderly patriarch asked, glancing around the clearing. Dressed in a bright-white shirt with red suspenders and checkered pants, he seemed both confused and color-blind.

"I don't think so, Ming," a female voice piped up. The woman, in her late thirties, wore a yoga outfit and TOMS shoes.

"Look at all the balloons. An entire arch of them," a middle-aged man with wide shoulders said.

In fact, balloon artists had spent hours configuring them this morning, in pleasing tones of purple and white. Anxious as he was, Winston had requested they come in a day early to make sure everything was ready beforehand. And they'd agreed, saying that the special liquid solution they sprayed into the balloons would keep them floating for days.

"Where exactly are we?" the broad-shouldered stranger continued. Frowning, he stared at the rest of his group, as though they *needed* to provide him with answers.

Kristy looked over at Winston, puzzled. "Relatives of yours?"

Winston shook his head. He'd never seen this odd bunch in his life.

Alex stiffened beside Winston. Then he marched over to the perplexed group with his arms wide open. "Ah, the Chans," he said. "Welcome to your Mystery Shack tour."

CHAPTER 4

ALEX INTRODUCED THE oddball group as the Chan family. The old man with red suspenders looked like he was in his seventies. The woman next to him, probably his wife, might have been a few years younger. Her hand clung to her husband's arm. She wore a polyester black dress printed in huge sunflowers and carried a large satchel. Winston wondered how she managed to stay upright with that giant leather bag weighing down her bony shoulder.

"Ming Chan," Alex said, pointing to the large purse belonging to the wife, "sells the finest in fashion carry-wear." Winston noticed that the rest of the family also carried bags. The men even had *murses*.

Winston's wedding party whispered among themselves, uncertain of what to do about the strangers, but nobody dared intervene.

The old man spoke again, his finger tapping his head. "Ming mean *bright* in Chinese. English name mean *smarts*." He beamed at those around him, showing off his yellow teeth and a chipped incisor.

Mrs. Chan spoke up, her voice tiny but sharp. "I'm Orchid, and my husband paid for this beautiful vacation." She waved her hand and gestured around the verdant area.

"Actually, the shack's in the back," Winston mumbled, but no one paid him any attention.

"Gorgeous," Mrs. Chan continued. "Special trip for the kids."

Winston counted seven offspring in all, and he wouldn't call them so young anymore. Every one of them looked at least thirty.

Winston glanced at Kristy. He leaned closer to her and whispered, "Should we do something to make them stop? They're interrupting our rehearsal."

Kristy shrugged. With her sweet nature, she'd probably let them carry on.

Mrs. Chan arranged her children by age. The oldest, the broad-shouldered man, shook off Mrs. Chan's hands as she touched him. "This is not a vacation. It's a work retreat," he said. "Meant to inspire us."

Mrs. Chan seemed oblivious to his disrespect. Or maybe she was hard of hearing. In any case, she started introducing the family. The oldest was named Fortune, or Fort for short.

How long would these niceties take? Winston caught Alex's eye and made a slashing motion across his neck.

His friend took the hint and interrupted Mrs. Chan. "Why don't we see the world-famous Mystery Shack now?"

The Chans finally left, some family members with looks of annoyance and others with joy. Winston breathed a sigh of relief. The schedule could go back to normal. He noticed that Kristy's smile returned, while Marcy's shoulders relaxed. The bridesmaids and groomsmen stood up straighter, and those watching the rehearsal repositioned themselves on their seats.

Winston turned his attention to the celebrant. "We don't need the best man to continue, right?"

"Nope, not for the rest of the rehearsal." The officiant shuffled the notes in his hands. "Now, where were we? Ah ha . . ."

The celebrant continued going over the schedule for the next day, and Winston couldn't wait for the whole thing to finish. Once the rehearsal was done, they'd booked a nice dinner for their friends and family at a great Malaysian place, Sambal. He could almost taste the curry dishes with their fragrant coconut milk, along with the fluffy layers of *roti canai* bread.

By the time he'd finished imagining the culinary delights, Alex had returned.

"All done?" Winston asked him. "They went off the property?"

"No, the Chans wanted to poke around the shack some more, but I came back as quick as I could. Best man duties." He gave Winston a thumbs-up. "Anyway, not like they can get lost in there."

They soon finished the rest of the rehearsal. Now calmer, Winston greeted the family and friends milling around the pasture. He gave his brother-in-law, Gary, a polite pat on the back. The guy better not hurt Marcy again—Winston felt protective of his older sis.

He issued an even cooler greeting to Carmen, Alex's girlfriend. Sure, she'd financed this amazing place, but he knew to be careful around the wannabe model; he'd been lured—and burned—by her a long time ago. Pete and Jazzman, his senior friends, he hugged with tenderness. They'd only grown closer over the years after their intense collaboration on Winston's big first case.

While discussing directions to the restaurant, he heard a faint noise. It grew louder, soon becoming a shrill scream. Winston distinguished a key word in the ongoing sharp cry: *help*.

CHAPTER 5

WINSTON AND ALEX rushed off to find out where the scream came from, leaving the celebrant in charge of calming the others down. They traced the sound to the Mystery Shack, its door flung wide open to the main room. Winston knew there was trouble when he peered inside and saw the Chan family gathered in a huddle, a few sobbing.

Alex burst into the shack. "What happened?"

The family members broke up their group. Orchid Chan shook her finger at Alex. "You're to blame."

Winston inched closer and saw someone lying on the floor. He peered at the figure. Old Mr. Chan, with his bright suspenders now in sharp contrast to his pale face.

"He collapsed," Mrs. Chan continued, "and fell down your stupid stairs to nowhere."

Winston addressed the family. "Does anyone here know CPR?" (Really, with all the elderly clients he had, Winston should've taken the course, but he'd never made the time.)

A woman in yoga wear looked at her brother. "Fort, didn't you take it?"

"It's been a while, Sandy." Fort's broad shoulders seemed to shrink down.

"Please try," Sandy urged.

So Fort went over to his dad and attempted resuscitation.

Winston saw Orchid's face twist in anger as she told Alex, "We'll sue you. Very dangerous. You should call this Danger Shack instead."

As they argued, Winston looked at the rest of the family. Sandy seemed focused on Fort's ministrations, trying to see if she could help revive their father. Besides her, he counted four other sons and another daughter.

One son stood in the distance, carrying a giant backpack, and staring out of a cobwebbed window. He was hunched over, and even from this distance, Winston could smell the overpowering menthol of a muscle rub ointment rolling off him. A different son rocked in a creaky old chair, surveying the scene with his jaw set and his lips pressed into a thin line. His grim face matched his all-black funereal attire. Another sat cross-legged in the middle of the glossy waxed floor trying to meditate during the disturbance.

One more son wearing a patchwork jacket wandered around the room with his hefty camera, oblivious and trying to take photos of the knickknacks on the shelves. The other daughter paced back and forth near the staircase to nowhere, sending off a waft of floral fragrance in her wake. She even wore a golden rose brooch on her shirt to match the scent.

Winston addressed the folks not involved with the CPR. "So, who called an ambulance?"

They looked at one another, aghast, pointing their fingers and asking, "Didn't you?" Finally, they singled out Mr. Muscle Rub to do it. Their brother Talent, nicknamed Tal.

"After all," the rose-scented woman said, "you're second oldest, next in line after Fort."

Ah, there was a pecking order, Winston thought. And Rose Princess appeared to be the youngest and at the bottom of the ladder. Even her gum-chewing habit pointed to her as the baby of the family.

Tal dialed while the youngest daughter blew a huge bubble and popped it right next to his ear.

"Stop it, Viv," Tal said.

She shrugged, spit the gum out into her palm, and dropped it in her purse.

Winston turned to the other siblings. "Is everyone all right? Can I get you anything?"

The photographer piped up. "Do you have a tripod? I forgot to pack mine."

"No, Lyle," the grim-faced one said. "Concentrate on what's going on. Ba's sick."

"He's seventy-five," Lyle said. "The guy needs rest, Bright."

"He's unconscious."

Lyle hazarded a glance at his father. "Napping," he concluded and continued snapping pictures of the room.

"Stepbrothers," Bright said. He extended his hand to Winston. "I'm Brighton, but everyone shortens my name."

Winston examined the big Chan family before him. "You guys aren't full-blooded siblings?"

"The Brady Bunch," Bright said. "I've got two stepbrothers, Evan and Lyle." He gestured to the meditating man and the photographer. "Plus, two stepsisters." He nodded at the girls.

"And those two are your brothers?" Winston pointed to the ones doing crucial work, CPR and calling the paramedics.

"Yeah, we care about Ba. Even if he is old and crotchety."

"So Mrs. Chan is your stepmom?"

"Right. Orchid. They married a year ago. Met on a senior cruise."

Their conversation stopped there because they heard the sirens.

When the paramedics arrived on the scene, they examined Ming. They checked his airway, their faces set like stone. "No breathing. We'll need to take him to the nearest hospital."

CHAPTER 6

O
RCHID CHAN, HER face haggard, insisted on accompanying her husband into the ambulance. She chased after the stretcher and acted quite the devoted newlywed. The remaining Chan members debated on who would steer their van to the hospital since they couldn't agree on the family's best driver.

"No, Fort's way too aggressive."

"Lyle's mind is always in the clouds. Doesn't pay attention to the road."

"Sandy's super slow."

Before they could decide, a police officer strode toward the Mystery Shack from the side path. As the cop got closer, Winston did a double take. "Officer Gaffey, what are you doing here?"

"Winston"—the policeman shook his head—"should have known you'd be around. Always causing trouble."

"I don't *initiate* things. I *investigate* them." Winston thought it was a clever use of words, but Gaffey grimaced.

"Leave crime solving to the professionals."

Winston hesitated for a second. Should he return to the rehearsal and trust Gaffey to do the job? But the sneer on the cop's face made Winston declare, "That's why I'm an official seniors' sleuth, a real expert."

Gaffey cocked an eyebrow. "Get your PI license yet?"

Winston felt his face heat up. He clenched his hands into fists. "Do *you* have a homicide detective badge?"

"Almost, actually." Gaffey gave a smug grin. "Taking the test real soon."

Winston's curiosity overcame his anger. "You what? When?"

Gaffey shrugged. "All these cases cropping up, someone's got to solve them."

"Why'd you get called in anyway?" Sure, the ambulance and firefighters had come, but they had deemed it an accident, not a crime scene.

"Noise disturbance," Gaffey said. "A neighbor complained, said she heard screaming."

Winston surveyed his surroundings. Acres of land around. Orchid Chan must have screamed pretty loud to have been heard by the adjacent homes.

Out of the corner of his eye, Winston noticed Fort making his way over. The eldest son introduced himself to Gaffey and said, "Officer, sorry you had to come out. Everything's okay now."

Gaffey pulled out a pad and pen. "What was the problem?"

Fort's bulky body towered over Gaffey and made the cop look like a scrawny teen. "My dad, he fell. And my stepmother lost it, screamed her head off."

Gaffey swiveled, looking at the family members around him. "Where is your father now? Is he okay?"

Tal's slouched figure ambled over. His accompanying taint of muscle rub must have reached Gaffey because the cop started gagging. The policeman pinched his nose closed for a moment.

"I called the ambulance for Ba," Tal informed Gaffey. "Fort did CPR."

Gaffey scribbled in his notebook. "How is your dad's health in general?"

"Better than mine." Tal rubbed his back and winced.

Fort took over the conversation. "He's seventy-five and in stable shape. Takes some pills."

"Name them," Gaffey said.

Fort threw his massive hands in the air. "I don't pay attention to that stuff . . . Sandy, come here."

The lululemon-clad lady walked over using long, smooth strides. "What do you need, Fort?"

"The officer wants to know about Ba's meds."

Sandy reached into the pocket of her yoga pants (they had pockets?) and pulled out a slim wallet. She opened it up and retrieved a laminated card. "All listed here," she said, handing it over to Gaffey.

Winston spied a few of the names: Lipitor, Coumadin . . .

After some furious writing, Gaffey returned the card to Sandy. "What medical problems does your dad have?"

"Cholesterol, high blood pressure . . . He even had a minor heart attack a few years back."

"He take all his meds today?" Gaffey asked. Winston had to give the cop props for asking a perceptive question. Maybe Gaffey would make a good detective someday.

Sandy wrinkled her brow and peeked into her wallet again. She wiggled out a miniature chore chart. "It was Viv's turn to oversee the meds this week."

Fort groaned. "She's the worst."

Sandy shushed him. "Bit of a prankster, but harmless," she confided to Winston and Gaffey. She whistled to get Viv's attention and called her over.

Viv sprang to action, almost twirling her way over to the group. "What's going on?"

Gaffey started waving his hand in front of his nose, no doubt to diffuse the wave of rose power that rolled toward him. "I need to know what pills you gave your dad today."

"The usual," she said. "I stuck them all in his pill box."

Winston stepped in. Time for him to shine and show Gaffey how to really investigate. Prove to the cop what kind of capable man Kristy would be marrying. "You don't remember the names?" Winston asked Viv.

"Nah, but maybe there was a yellow one?"

Winston glanced over at Sandy, who patted Viv's head like a child.

"You did follow the Google doc, right?" Sandy asked her sister.

Viv nodded. "Every last detail."

Sandy told Winston and Gaffey, "We keep the medication names, colors, and dosages in the cloud."

The other brothers saw the group talking and headed over. Bright came with his dark attire, Lyle with his huge camera, and even Evan stopped *om*-ing and joined the conversation. The men turned to Gaffey and started firing off questions, wondering if everything was okay, if there would be an investigation.

Gaffey closed his notebook and put away his pen. "No, I don't think so. Seems like everything's fine. Your dad probably had a medical scare, but the doctors will take good care of him."

Winston noticed looks of relief on their faces. Even he felt calmer by Gaffey's soothing prediction—until he heard some loud popping from outside the shack. Sounded like machine gun fire. And it must have come from the clearing.

"Kristy!" he exclaimed and started sprinting.

CHAPTER 7

WINSTON HUFFED ALL the way to the clearing, with Gaffey following right behind. Once he found Kristy, Winston hugged her tight. He felt her tremble in his arms. "Are you okay, sweetheart?"

In his peripheral vision, Winston noticed the cop scanning the scene, one hand resting on his police gear belt.

"I'm fine," Kristy told Winston, touching his cheek with gentle fingers.

"But I heard a gun." Winston looked around him. Everything seemed to be in order, and none of the guests appeared injured.

"Oh no, nothing like that," she said. "We all froze until the noise ended. Nobody got hurt, but I can still hear ringing." She rubbed at her ears.

Gaffey joined them, and Winston restrained from scowling at the cop for ruining the intimate moment.

"Kristy," the policeman said, softening his tone at her name.

She looked at Gaffey. Winston saw the cop freeze, noticed the man almost stop breathing. It must be Kristy's exquisiteness, that emerald dress highlighting her natural fresh beauty.

Kristy pulled Winston close to her as she spoke. "Thank goodness my groom-to-be came to protect me . . . But what are you doing here, Mark?"

Gaffey looked back and forth between the two of them. "You're really getting married? I thought my great-aunt was joking. And to that guy?" He jerked his thumb at Winston.

Winston looped his arm around Kristy's waist. "The big day is tomorrow."

"I still don't understand," Kristy said, addressing Gaffey, whose mouth had dropped open. "Why did you come to the wedding rehearsal?"

Gaffey shook his head a few times, maybe to clear it. "Got a call, neighborhood disturbance. Some screaming."

Kristy shuddered. "I heard it." Her gaze dropped down to the green grass at her feet. "From the shack, right? Was it the Chan family?"

Winston nodded. He wanted to draw her even closer as he spoke his next words. "The father had a fall. An ambulance took him to the hospital. Mrs. Chan's with him right now."

Kristy wrung her hands. Her elegant fingers twisted together. "I wish I could do something for them."

Always so sweet. She thought of everyone else first. "What about the scare here?" Winston asked. "I want to make sure you're okay."

Kristy shrugged it off. "That was nothing. A few balloons got popped on the wedding arch."

Marcy swooped in at this point. "More than just a couple." She sighed and gestured to a space beyond the clearing, hidden behind some towering trees. "The whole arch is gone. Only the frame is left."

"They're just balloons," Kristy said.

Winston could see Marcy switch into problem-solving mode. A frown spread across her face. "This wedding will be *perfect* if I have anything to do with it."

Marcy narrowed her eyes at Gaffey. "Officer," she said, giving him a brief head nod. His sister didn't have any lost love for the cop, not after he'd come so late to the crime scene during the Magnolia Lane case.

Kristy bit her lips. They were a sweet pink color. "I would be able to concentrate more on the balloons if I knew someone was taking care of the Chans."

Gaffey shifted his feet to a wider stance. "I'll escort their car to the hospital. With sirens blaring, they'll get there in no time."

Kristy gave the cop a grateful smile, and Winston felt his stomach roil. Without thinking, he piped up. "And I'll drive them to the hospital. None of them are in the right frame of mind to handle a car right now."

Kristy turned to Winston, her smile growing wider. She gave him a peck on the cheek. "You're the best," she said. "Now, I won't worry at all. Once you finish, head over to the restaurant, and we can enjoy our rehearsal dinner."

Winston touched his forehead against hers. The silky strands of her hair tickled his ears. "I'll see you soon."

Turning around, Winston noticed a sullen look on Gaffey's face. But then the cop rearranged his features into an impassive look. Without saying anything, Gaffey marched off in the direction of the Mystery Shack.

CHAPTER 8

WINSTON AND GAFFEY showed up around the same time at the Mystery Shack and informed the Chan family about their plan. Everyone thanked them for helping.

Fort took charge and told Winston that he'd ride shotgun in the car to provide directions.

"Follow me to our parking spot," he said to Winston, but his hand gesture encompassed all his siblings. They trailed after Fort's hulk of a build, with Winston at the rear a few paces behind. Huffing under his breath, Winston cursed the Buddha belly he possessed.

Winston examined the dirty van parked at the curb. The white exterior paint had faded away, and it now showed a dull gray from the layer underneath. To add insult to injury, a flock of birds seemed to have used the car for target practice.

Winston slid into the driver's seat and wrinkled his nose. The whole car reeked of corn chips and sweat. He also noticed a mass of bug bodies smeared across the windshield. "Did you drive all the way here?" he asked Fort, who'd buckled in next to him.

"Yep. San Gabriel Valley in Los Angeles."

"A long drive?" Winston asked as he adjusted the seat and mirrors.

"Six hours with these guys?" Fort jerked his thumb back at the rest of the family. "Not my idea of a joyride."

Winston peeked over his shoulder to make sure everyone had settled into the back of the van. "Don't you all run a business? Work together every day? I figured you'd be a solid family unit."

Fort grunted. "Some of us do more than others at the job." He glared at Bright behind him, and his brother frowned. The grim look Bright gave Fort matched the funereal black he wore.

Tal spoke up. "We run different areas of the business." He rubbed his forehead as he spoke. Winston hoped the man wouldn't spread muscle rub there by accident, too. That would not help the already stuffy odor in the vehicle.

Winston started the engine and tried to turn on the AC, to no avail. Instead, he rolled down the windows. Maybe the slight breeze as they drove along would cleanse the air.

The silence in the car grew heavier by the minute. Winston could almost feel the weight of anxiety from all the passengers stuck in the cramped van.

Though Fort had claimed the role of navigator, the man stared out the window with a blank gaze. It didn't matter. Gaffey's flashing lights blazed an easy trail for Winston to follow.

To lighten the atmosphere, Winston asked the group, "So, how's your vacation been so far? Er, besides this incident . . ."

"Vacation?" Fort turned his attention from the window and to Winston. "Don't you know? This is a work retreat for us."

Winston frowned. "But your mom said—"

Tal groaned, and Winston looked over to see him hunch in his seat and smack his forehead with vigorous slaps. "To set things straight, Orchid's our stepmom."

"Oh, right. She's mom to"—Winston ticked the names off—"Sandy, Evan, Lyle, and Viv."

"Us alpha males," Fort said, "are from a better set of genes."

Winston heard snorts from the others in the van. "I stand corrected. This trip is for work?"

Sandy answered first. "Correct."

Peeking in the rearview mirror, Winston saw her stretch into a pose. Could she do yoga even strapped into a car?

She continued, "Ming wanted us to get inspired by the Mystery Shack. We drove all the way from LA to see it."

Winston paused with his hands at the ten-and-two position on the wheel. "You mean to say your vacation is *all* about seeing that measly shack?"

Lyle held up his camera. "It was beautiful. So weird and wonderful. I got a few amazing snaps."

Winston scratched the back of his neck. Should he tell them? Pricked by his conscience, he said, "There's actually a larger and more authentic version. It's called the Winchester Mystery House."

"Of course there is," Evan said. He didn't seem ruffled by Winston's words. Maybe his constant meditation kept him on an even keel.

Winston should ask him for tips before the big day tomorrow. "You're so calm about this info."

"We know the shack's a fake," Evan said.

Winston heard Viv blowing bubbles. She must have pulled out some gum during the ride. "Yeah," she said. "Ming does this often, shows us different kinds of knockoffs."

Hmm, strange. But maybe . . . "Is it some sort of family bonding ritual then?" Winston asked.

Fort guffawed and elbowed Winston in the ribs. He cried out in pain and almost lost control of the car.

At the last minute, Winston corrected the steering wheel. His ribs would definitely hurt during the ceremony tomorrow.

"What's so funny?" Winston asked.

Sandy stretched around her seatbelt and yoga'ed her way to holding a feathered purse in his peripheral vision. "The whole trip was to see if we'd be inspired to create a new line of goods. We make fakes."

Bright grumbled. "Without quality material."

Evan sighed and said, "And all the employees are paid so little."

Fort shushed his brothers. "We make genuine knockoff bags." An oxymoron, but Winston let it go.

They were almost at the hospital now. He could see the building at the road's corner and took a quick glance at the lot. Mostly full, but he was a master of the parking roulette. Confident of his ability, he pulled into the lot and asked, "So, was the Mystery Shack inspirational?"

"Yeah," Fort replied. "I'm thinking we could build a mini Taj Mahal."

Viv groaned. "What about fragrances instead? A different one for every mood." She spritzed on some more of her rose perfume, and Winston stifled the urge to sneeze. Good thing he'd spied an open spot. He couldn't park the car fast enough.

While Winston turned off the engine, Tal said, "I don't know. How can we work even more than we already do? Build something new? Everyone's taxed, and Ba needs to retire soon."

"If he survives," Bright said.

Viv shot him a miffed look.

"Life and death. Part of the same cycle."

Time to go before a fight broke out. Winston unlocked the doors. They all shuffled into the hospital in a somber mood.

CHAPTER 9

THE HOSPITAL GLARED white when they entered the facility. Maybe the clean vibe would inspire hope in the Chan family. Winston looked around the expansive space, trying to figure out where to go or who to ask.

Gaffey was one step ahead of him, already approaching what looked like an information desk. Fort must have seen the policeman, too, because he soon joined the cop. At the desk, Fort started talking, but the receptionist appeared flustered.

Except for Fort, the other Chans seemed confused and uncertain about what to do. A few of them moved closer to Winston, while others roamed the lobby. He guessed a hospital visit wasn't on the checklist for their work retreat.

Suddenly, an annoying sharp whistle sounded, and Winston looked around to find the source. Covering his ears, he noticed

Gaffey pulling his fingers away from his mouth. None of the other patients and visitors dared comment on the cop's behavior, probably because they saw his uniform.

Gaffey called out, "Come on." He beckoned to the Chan family.

"You, too, driver," he said to Winston.

They followed Gaffey to a set of elevators and crowded inside a lift. Once they arrived at the appropriate floor, they filed into a small waiting room.

The walls were gray, and the painted prints on them uninspired. The chairs were empty except for Orchid sitting in the corner, crying. Mascara ran down her face, although she tried to wipe away the mess when she noticed them.

She stood up and looked at Gaffey. "Officer, what are you doing here?"

"Call me Mark," he said. "I escorted your family to the hospital. I knew it'd be quicker with my patrol car leading the way."

She blinked at him. "How do you even know about my husband's fall?"

"Ah, I got called to the shack on account of a noise disturbance. A woman screaming."

Orchid swiped at her eyes. "My husband, he fell down the stairs. Too terrible."

Orchid's biological children moved in and fluttered around her, but Winston noticed her stepkids kept their distance. The odd family dynamics made the hair on the back of his neck rise, but he shook away the icy feeling.

After her kids ministered to Orchid, she calmed down. She turned to Winston. "Why aren't you at your wedding rehearsal?"

"My fiancée asked me to help your family, so I drove the van." Winston gave himself a mental pat on the back. He made a sweeping gesture that encompassed the Chan children. "Nobody could agree on who should drive."

A hint of irritation crept into Orchid's voice. "Figures," she said, giving Fort a disgusted look. "Second in command, and you can't even lead."

Fort balled his hands into fists, moving to tower over his stepmother. "I'm not here for your criticism. How is Ba doing?"

"He's . . ." Orchid sighed and sat back down in her chair. She slumped.

Evan whispered a few mantras to her. Sandy went over to the nearby water cooler and filled up a thin paper cup. Lyle tried to place his arm around Orchid's shoulder without bumping his camera into her. Viv sat down next to Orchid and held her mother's hands.

Winston wanted to jump in and say something empathetic. He moved near Orchid and spoke in a soft voice. "This must be hard for you. I understand Ming was going to retire soon."

Instead of calming her, his words made Orchid burst into tears. She dropped Viv's hand and covered her face with her palms. Viv stared at her rejected fingers, her hand perched awkwardly on the chair's armrest.

"Why'd you say that to her?" Tal whispered to Winston, pulling out a handkerchief and handing it to Orchid.

While she blew her nose, Gaffey raised his eyebrows at Winston. The cop pointed at Winston's shoe and then Winston's lips. Winston's face grew hot.

Winston needed to heal Orchid's mood, help her feel better. "I'm sure it'll turn out all right in the end," he said. "Before you know it, you'll be going on your senior cruises and travels after he recovers."

Orchid sniffed. "I hope so. We did want to do one of those China tours—the ones where you wake up bright and early each day."

The super deals where you go off to the major sights, crammed with buying "opportunities" throughout the trip. Winston got flyers in the mail from those tour companies all the time.

Orchid blew her nose with one big honk on the handkerchief. "The doctor will come out soon. They didn't tell me much in the beginning. Or maybe I couldn't understand. Too much information being thrown at me."

Gaffey remained standing, but Winston and the others decided to sit down. On the hard, plastic chairs. He thought the hospital could have afforded better furniture, knowing that family members and friends might be sitting for a long time. He looked around at the Chan children to see how they were coping with the uncomfortable seats.

Some of them seemed frozen: Fort overflowed in his chair, Bright appeared a grim statue, Evan achieved a Zen state, and Sandy perched cross-legged. The others kept fidgeting: Tal pulled a mini-massager out of his murse, Lyle flipped through photos on his camera, and Viv blew giant bubbles with her gum.

Finally, the doctor came. He looked weary as he entered and made a straight line to Orchid. "Your husband's still unconscious and in critical condition, Mrs. Chan." The doctor rubbed at the stubble on his chin. "You'll have to wait some more, I'm afraid."

Orchid's voice cracked. "How much longer?"

"I'm not sure." The doctor glanced at the wall clock. "But I advise getting some food in your stomach."

That's when Winston's phone rang: "Chances Are." His special ringtone for Kristy. The doctor wagged his finger at Winston before he headed out, pointing at a sign that read, "Silence your cell phones." Oops.

Winston moved over to the side of the room for a bit of privacy. "Everything okay?"

"Lovely. Your sister's gone to the store to buy extra balloons. What about on your end?"

"Sadly, Mr. Chan's in critical condition. No word on how long of a wait. In fact, the doctor told Mrs. Chan she should probably get something to eat—"

"Perfect. That's what we'll do then," Kristy said.

"Huh?"

"Invite them to our rehearsal dinner. Marcy can drive your car while you take the Chans. I'll call the restaurant right now. I'm sure they won't mind more customers."

"But our budget . . ." Winston tried to calculate the figures in his head, but Kristy was better with finances.

"Don't worry, it'll work out," she said. "Which hospital are you at?"

"San Jose Central."

"Great, that's close to Sambal. Feeding them is the least we can do during their time of difficulty."

Winston sucked air in through his teeth. "Okay, so that will be an extra eight people."

"Nine," she said.

"I think you miscounted. Mr. Chan needs to stay in the hospital."

"No, there's someone else. Go and invite—"

"Uh-uh. I don't think so."

"Mark deserves it. He was so kind to them."

Winston glanced over at the cop who hovered nearby. Gaffey must have overheard the conversation because his face erupted in a huge grin. Winston couldn't back out now and show tension in his relationship with Kristy. "Fine."

"Thank you, Winston." She made a smooching noise.

Winston hoped the phone kiss would fortify him for the upcoming crazy dinner.

CHAPTER 10

WINSTON INVITED THE Chan family for dinner at Sambal. The younger generation readily agreed, but Orchid hesitated. "We should wait here," she said.

Fort shook his head. "Ba won't even notice."

Sandy placed a hand on her mom's shoulder. "Fort's right. And you look exhausted. Even the doctor told us to get dinner."

Orchid nodded. "Maybe you're right."

Mrs. Chan tagged behind them as they left the waiting room and exited the hospital. On the sidewalk outside, Winston said, "I can drive the family."

Orchid shook her head. "You don't have to. I'm sure you're swamped with wedding details."

"No, I don't mind."

"Where is the restaurant?"

Winston told her the major cross streets but soon realized she wouldn't be familiar with the San Jose area. He pulled out his phone to map out the route. Before he could punch in his passcode, Orchid pointed at the words on his screensaver. "What's that mean? Seniors' Sleuth?"

"My job title. I'm a detective."

She frowned while he unlocked his phone and opened up the map application. Peeking over his shoulder, she said, "I think I can get there myself. Hand over the keys."

"It's really no problem."

She kept her palm out, waiting. It would be like nailing jelly to convince her not to drive, so he deposited the keys into her hand.

"I can ride in the back, though, and help navigate."

She motioned for Gaffey to come over. "Winston, you go sit with the nice officer. More room in his car anyway."

Orchid left Winston without a backward glance. The rest of the Chan family followed her, and Fort slapped Winston on the back as he passed. "No problem. I mapped the place out. She won't get lost."

Winston turned his attention to Gaffey as he watched the Chans pile into their old van. He wasn't worried about the matriarch anymore. Instead, he shuffled after Gaffey with plodding steps. Could the two of them survive a car ride together?

The cop stopped at the rear door of his patrol car, and Winston's heart rate soared. Would the man be so mean as to lock him in the back during the drive?

Gaffey snickered and held his hands up. "Kidding," he said. "Go in the passenger's side."

Winston complied and buckled up. Tight. No knowing what kind of driving maneuvers Gaffey would make.

He gave the restaurant's address to Gaffey and stayed silent for the first few minutes of the ride, but the quiet soon grew on his nerves. Why wasn't Gaffey turning on the radio? Fine, he'd find something neutral to talk about. "Sad about Mr. Chan," Winston said.

Gaffey shrugged. "It's normal. A heart attack for an old man is quite common."

Winston thought about one of his regular senior clients, an ex-Marine who still tore up the gym. "Some people are still in the prime of their health, even at eighty."

"Not Mr. Chan . . . or so Fort told me."

Winston turned his attention to Gaffey, gazing at the cop's profile. "He say something to you?"

"Not directly. He was trying to talk to the gal at the info desk. Wanted to tell her his dad's been through some heart complications, even has a DNR. Tried to outline Ming's wishes to her."

Winston tapped his fingers against the dash, thinking.

Gaffey threw him an irritated look. "Stop that noise."

"Sorry." He stilled his fingers. "Do you remember what Fort said? Details about the DNR?"

Gaffey kept his eyes on the road, speeding through a yellow light with ease. "Something along the lines of his dad not wanting to be a vegetable, that the family could pull the plug if needed."

"I wonder," Winston said. "Was it natural for Mr. Chan to collapse like that?"

Gaffey snorted. "Detecting is messing with your head. Remember, I talked to the family, and they said the old man had suffered a heart attack before. Murphy's Law."

"You mean Occam's razor. The simplest solution is usually correct," Winston said as they neared the restaurant. "Murphy's Law means the worst thing that can happen does."

"Whatever, Mr. Spock," Gaffey said as they pulled into a parking spot right in front of Sambal's large plate-glass window. Had Gaffey just complimented Winston? He wasn't quite sure.

From the parked car, Winston noticed his friends and family staring at them through the window. His eyes located his bride-to-be. Kristy, in her beautiful emerald dress, waved at them. Winston felt a goofy grin spreading across his face.

Beside him, Gaffey muttered, "Yeah, Murphy's Law."

"You don't have to come in," Winston said.

"But I'm wanted here." Gaffey groomed himself using the rearview mirror. "She invited me."

Winston counted to ten in his head to calm down.

CHAPTER 11

WINSTON LEFT GAFFEY to preen in the car. As he opened the door to the restaurant, he noticed the Chan van pull into the parking lot. He decided not to wait for them because the smell of curry wafted toward him, making his mouth salivate.

He went over to Kristy and his friends seated at a long rectangular table. Twelve similar tables filled the dining area, and against the far wall, Sambal offered a bar that served exotic Asian drinks.

The configuration of the long tables in the dining room made for awkward moving around Sambal. It required dodging other people when trying to get to the restrooms, but at least large groups could sit together.

Kristy motioned for Winston to sit next to her. She pointed at the whole coconut pierced with a straw placed on a nearby placemat. Looked like she'd thought about him and already ordered one of his favorite drinks.

He couldn't wait for the refreshing taste of the coconut water. Maybe it would take away the bitterness left by Mrs. Chan's brush-off, and also overcome the sourness left by a car ride with Gaffey.

Winston gave Kristy a quick hug before he sat next to her. She smelled like sweetness itself. A hint of gardenia floated off her skin and intoxicated him.

Snatching the drink in front of him, he began gulping down the coconut water. Then he followed through with the niceties, greeting his two future brothers-in-law. One of Kristy's brothers was single, but the other was married and had a toddler.

The little boy clapped his hands at Winston, and he smiled at the tyke. Huh. Maybe he could be a dad someday . . . with the perfect woman by his side. He squeezed Kristy's hand, and she rubbed her thumb over his palm in return.

Carmen and Alex greeted him, his best man toasting him with a glass of bubbly. Did they usually serve champagne at Malaysian restaurants? Or maybe the couple had slipped in some BYOB by paying an extra fee. Money sure made things easier.

His Sweet Breeze friends greeted him, too. Anastasia wiggled her jewel-laden fingers at him while Jazzman tipped his top hat. Pete offered a small head nod.

Only Marcy frowned at Winston, followed by a prolonged look at her Rolex. Since she happened to be sitting on the other side of Winston, and he didn't want her to start in on him, he explained his tardiness. "It took some time to get things settled at the hospital."

Marcy's husband, Gary, who sat on her other side, placed an arm over her shoulder. "Give Winston a break," he said, pecking Marcy on the cheek. Looked like their relationship was on the mend. Winston grinned, knowing that his own romance with Kristy had reignited his sister's previously faltering marriage.

Kristy leaned over and whispered in his ear. "Everything okay with the Chans?"

Winston shook his head. "They almost didn't come, but—
"

At that moment, the door made a loud swishing sound. Gaffey kept it open with a gallant gesture of his hands and ushered the Chan family inside.

They streamed in like a sinuous snake and made their way over to Winston's table. He frowned. Why had that particular image cropped up?

Orchid paused in front of Winston and Kristy. "Thank you for dinner," she said.

Then on seeing Alex at the table, she glared at him.

He made a clucking noise with his tongue. "It's a shame about your husband's accident."

"Those stairs in the Mystery Shack are dangerous. I could sue the two of you."

Carmen lifted her glass of champagne up. "Not after signing our detailed contract. No liability, remember?"

Orchid huffed and turned her back on them. She fumed, and Winston was glad he wasn't the source of her displeasure this time. Her anger filled the air, choking the previous joyous mood.

Kristy invited the family to sit down, leave their worries behind, and enjoy the food. She placed a hand on Orchid's back and guided her to a seat next to Pete. Hopefully, the vet would turn on his more charming side today. Or maybe they could commiserate about the trials of life together.

The rest of the Chan family then divided themselves around the long table, and Lyle ended up next to Jazzman. The two of them could talk about the arts. After all, didn't Jazzman put up framed photos in his room? Winston could see Lyle already flipping through images on his camera and showing them to Jazzman, their heads bent over the device.

Once the Chans sat down, Winston breathed a sigh of relief. He realized that Gaffey's chivalrous door opening would ensure that the cop get the last spot, a seat far from the center of the table where Winston sat.

Winston had drunk over half of his coconut water by the time the waitress appeared at their table. She wore a traditional dark-blue batik dress with many swirls adorning it. Her hair was pinned up, and a white plumeria perched behind her ear. Without needing to glance at the menu, he and Kristy put in the order for their celebratory dinner.

The waitress wrote everything down and then asked for people's drink preferences. Most of the Chans stuck with water, but Orchid opted for *teh tarik*, the pulled milk tea. And Fort asked for a coffee.

"Caffeine doesn't affect me," he boasted. "I can drink five cups a day. Keeps my energy flowing."

The waitress bustled away but came back within minutes, balancing a huge tray. She doled out the glasses of water and two steaming mugs.

"Do you have sugar?" Fort asked after he'd been served.

"On the table," she said. Satisfied that everyone had their beverage of choice, she turned to Winston and said, "Now let me check on your food."

After the waitress whisked away, Viv leaned across the table and dangled a spoonful of white grains in front of Fort's nose. "Got your sugar for you, *dai gor*."

Fort leaned back in his chair and practically put his feet up. "That's right. I'm the big brother, and the youngest should always serve the eldest."

She made her voice lilt. "Of course, Fort, my dear big brother." Then she dumped the spoon's contents into his coffee and stirred.

Fort licked his lips. Upon his first sip, he spat the drink onto the table and at the person across from him—Orchid.

His stepmom let out a few choice curse words in Cantonese before excusing herself to the ladies' room.

Fort pointed to the offending drink and accused Viv. "You put salt in my coffee."

"Oops, couldn't tell the difference."

Lyle stopped showing pictures to Jazzman for a minute and piped up. "But the salt's in a bottle, and the sugar's in packets."

"Prankster." Fort gnashed his teeth and glared at Viv, even as Orchid returned to the table. "You probably even 'forgot' to give Ba his pills, and that's why he collapsed."

"Stop spouting lies." Viv took a napkin and mopped up the coffee mess on the table. "And look who's talking . . . you're the next in line to inherit." She tossed the sodden napkin onto his lap.

Why would the Chan family even joke about Ming's fall? Winston shuddered.

Fort looked shocked. He spluttered and let the cloth napkin slide to the floor. He also signaled for the waitress to return and asked for a new coffee.

Thank goodness Winston's own family wasn't so dysfunctional. It had been rough losing their parents, but through it all, he and his sister loved each other.

Turning to Marcy, he asked her about the latest herbology research. She gave a brain dump, and her use of scientific plant names, along with Gary's rhythmic *uh-huhs* by her side, lulled Winston into a dazed state of boredom.

Only the smell of bread from the *roti* platter woke up his brain. Winston reached out to take one and split the fluffy, layered appetizer with his beautiful bride-to-be. Kristy flashed him a smile before resuming an intense game of peek-a-boo with her nephew.

Winston dipped his piece of roti into the fragrant curry and looked at Kristy playing with the little boy. She'd make an excellent mother. As he nibbled the bread and continued watching them, both his stomach and his heart felt an immense burst of joy.

Then a giant thump resounded. The table gave a small vibration.

Fort pounded his fist again on the wood and stood up in haste. "Get that away from me!"

Winston looked to where Fort pointed.

CHAPTER 12

WINSTON SAW FORT trembling before the satay plate. The skewered meat looked delicious to Winston, the chunks of beef crisscrossed with grill lines mesmerizing. Its tantalizing scent made his mouth water. The chef had even prettied the dish with a sprinkle of peanuts over the kebabs. Garnishes of cucumber gave a splash of color, and a ramekin with creamy peanut sauce nestled next to the meat.

It was almost comical watching the broad-shouldered man quake with fear. "Peanuts." Fort's eyes widened. "I'm allergic."

Viv picked up a stick. "Oh, you mean this?" She brandished the meat at Fort, her skinny arm waving it before his face.

"Not funny," Tal said. "He's *deathly* allergic."

"Only if he eats it." Her shoulders slumped. "Besides, it's just a joke." She dropped her arm and took a bite of the satay.

Tal muttered under his breath and called over the waitress. He ordered a unique drink, a bottle of *baijiu*, known as "Chinese firewater."

Kristy leaned over the table toward Fort. "You do have an EpiPen, right?"

Fort frowned. "Left it at the motel."

Kristy bit her lip. Her forehead crinkled, and Winston squeezed her shoulder to reassure her.

"We'll move the dish," he said. "It's the only one we ordered that has peanuts."

Winston put the juicy platter far from Fort, but Lyle spoke up. "Can I see it a sec?"

Lyle lifted his camera. "I want to do an Instagram post."

"Pass it around," Tal said, his usual dark manner brightening at the sight of the yummy appetizer. "We're starving here. Don't worry, we'll get rid of the dish soon enough, so Fort can relax."

The satay got passed around to everyone except Fort. People all seemed to snatch up a stick with quick hands. Before he knew it, Winston ended up with the empty dish in front of him. He asked the waitress to come back and pick up all the finished appetizer platters.

As she lifted the plate with roti crumbs on it, Winston remembered to take the curry dip. He also tried to grab the peanut sauce on the other plate, but it was missing. Someone else must love condiments like he did.

The waitress cleared everything, and then Marcy clinked her glass with a fork. She raised her drink and toasted. "To Winston and Kristy: May your marriage be loving and long-lasting."

Cheers erupted around the table, and Winston grinned. Glasses clinked, and Winston turned his attention to Kristy. "Can you believe it? Tomorrow we'll be husband and wife."

She smiled up at him, and her utter focus made him feel faint with love. "I can't wait."

He tucked a wayward strand of hair behind her ears and stared into her eyes.

She stroked his cheek. Then she lifted her left hand, showing off the diamond on her ring finger. It sparkled in the soft lighting of the restaurant.

They chatted about their honeymoon plans. Marcy had gifted them with a trip to exotic Tahiti. They lost themselves in a luxurious conversation about bungalows hovering above glittering water. Soon, though, Winston could hear a rising burble of angry Cantonese from down the table.

Then a sharp cry of "*sau seng*" came from Orchid and shattered their dreamy talking. Why would the matriarch be saying "shut up?"

Winston noticed the members of the Chan family staring each other down. Their anger seemed divided by gender, with the women glaring at the men.

Winston glanced at Marcy, needing a translation. His knowledge of simple Cantonese words didn't help him decipher lengthy conversations. "Family troubles," she mouthed. Was his rehearsal dinner going to turn into a brawl? Maybe he shouldn't have invited the Chans despite Kristy's suggestion.

Before he had a chance to intervene, Evan said, "Let's take it down a notch. I'll lead us in a few tranquil breathing exercises." He spoke about emptying the mind and focusing on the present, on deep breaths. By the time the main dishes came out, everyone had calmed down enough to eat a civil dinner.

CHAPTER 13

THE MAIN ENTREES came out, and people oohed and aahed at the food. Winston had ordered a feast to celebrate: curry crab, mango chicken, garlic kangkong vegetables. He indulged in the curry's spiciness tempered by rich coconut milk, along with a battle between sweet and savory spices of the other dishes.

In between eating, he turned his attention to Kristy's brothers to make small talk. After all, he hoped to be a close-knit family starting tomorrow. One of them worked in the computer industry (hardware), so they talked about processing speed and microchips. The other one did banking but talked only of his "genius" toddler son—how the boy could stack blocks into a pyramid and knew basic words in three different languages.

Finally, the dessert came. Individual servings of *bo bo cha cha* were put out in front of each place setting. Winston looked at the coconut milk dessert brimming with delicious ingredients like sweet potatoes, taro, and tapioca jellies.

Everyone decided to dig in. Winston saw a flurry of hands grabbing bowls. Shiny spoons flashed in the air. He was also about to follow suit when Kristy placed her hand over his. Her grasp prevented him from grabbing a spoon. "The gifts," she whispered.

Oh, right. They'd gotten presents for the bridesmaids and groomsmen. He was supposed to shower the bridal party with appreciation according to some wedding planning website Kristy had pored over.

Winston cleared his throat. "Thank you for coming tonight. Kristy and I are grateful to have close family and friends supporting us. As a token of our gratitude, we bought gifts for—"

Loud music blared down the table. It was a heart-stopping rendition of "Eye of the Tiger." Winston saw Orchid fish the phone out from her purse and listen.

"Yes, I'm Mrs. Chan," she yelled into the receiver.

Winston threw his hands in the air and gave up talking. Kristy patted his shoulder and handed out wrapped presents to her bridesmaids. She had decided on refined gifts for the ladies. The women received amethyst bracelets, which matched the color of their dresses.

Kristy motioned to Winston for him to hand out his picks to the men. Inspired by his inner geek, he'd selected joystick-shaped cufflinks. As he passed out his gifts to the proper recipients, he noticed Orchid with the phone to her ear, frozen.

When she finally moved, Orchid collapsed in her chair. She pushed away her finished plate and sunk her head in her arms. Then she wept.

Viv leaned over her mother. "What's the matter?"

"Ming," Orchid replied. "He's dead."

CHAPTER 14

THE NEWS OF Mr. Chan's death shocked everyone at the table. Winston's friends muttered variations of "What a shame" while Kristy's brothers shook their heads. Kristy herself got up and stood next to Orchid to hold her hand.

It's just like Kristy, Winston thought, to worry about other people during our wedding rehearsal dinner. How did his fiancée feel? Could she be rattled as well? He got up and placed an arm around her waist.

On the other hand, Orchid looked terrible. She stared down at her phone with a baffled expression, her face ashen. However, the reactions from the adult kids varied.

The biological sons of Mr. Chan seemed troubled. Fort slammed his fist into the table, rattling the plates and cups. Tal gazed into his unopened bottle of baijiu, appearing to contemplate its contents. Bright folded his arms across his chest and looked down, seeming to fade into a dark humor that matched his pitch-black outfit.

The stepchildren showed mixed reactions. Sandy started trembling, and Winston could hear her deep centering breaths hard at work. Evan closed his eyes and seemed to tune out the whole world. Lyle dropped his camera but didn't notice. Viv wrung her hands.

Then she started in on an explanation. "It must have been his heart, already weak from the last attack."

Fort shook his fist in the air. "Told Ba he worked too hard. Said I could take over earlier."

"We should've had a real vacation," Tal said, "like I wanted." He scowled at his full bottle of baijiu.

Orchid's head snapped up. "*Aiyaa.* I asked him to retire sooner. Said we could pass the business on and relax."

Lyle shook his head, retrieved his camera, and checked its inner workings.

Sandy's breathing became more labored, and her lips tightened. "I hate the company."

The whole family stared at her. Winston couldn't tell if they were more troubled by her words or her unusual lack of composure.

Evan opened his eyes and placed his hand on his sister's shoulder. "I agree with Sandy. Time to end the practice of underpaying employees . . . "

The whole family erupted in a clamor, seeming to verbally spar with one another. A cacophony of strident voices filled the air. Winston could only make out a few select phrases:

"Need living wages."

"At least they're employed."

"What does the Chan name stand for?"

Their waitress edged to the table and crept over to Winston's side. "If you could pay now, sir . . . " She gave him the bill and scurried away.

Winston decided to skip using his credit card. The faster he left, the better. And the other customers at Sambal were starting to give their table dirty looks. He paid in cash, leaving a large tip.

Projecting his voice, he addressed those seated around him. "Thank you for coming to our rehearsal dinner. It's getting late, and we'd better leave."

Everybody focused on Winston as he spoke. The squabbling stopped. Most of the group rose from their chairs and gathered their belongings. A few, though, spooned up the last bits of their *bo bo cha cha*. Fort finished his dessert *and* chugged down the remains of his coffee.

 Immediately, he started coughing. Fort's face turned red as he clutched his throat.

Abandoning her post by Orchid's side, Kristy rushed over to Fort. After a moment's observation, she said, "He's having trouble breathing."

What was wrong? It must be—"His peanut allergy," Winston said.

Kristy scanned the dining room full of patrons and asked, "Does anyone have an EpiPen?"

Nobody did. Fort continued to make choking noises, and Winston flagged down the waitress. "Call nine-one-one," he said.

CHAPTER 15

WHEN THE AMBULANCE came, Fort was taken to the closest hospital. It happened to be the same one his father had been in. Another tragic accident for the Chan family. If Winston had been superstitious, he'd say the Chans were cursed.

As it were, his mind churned away, trying to figure out the puzzle. Ming, the patriarch, dying—what would that mean for the Chan family?

Thinking like a detective, he needed to unearth info from every family member, but what about Kristy? He felt torn, wanting to indulge his thirst for sleuthing while also feeling devoted to his lovely fiancée. Besides, this weekend should be about them and their future life together, right?

Kristy sidled next to him. "You want to understand what's happening."

He nodded. How well she knew him.

"Figure it out," she said. "I need my beauty sleep anyway."

Her permission proved again that he was marrying the right gal. He kissed her on the forehead. "Thank you, Kristy."

She gave him a sweet smile. "Have fun sleuthing."

Winston thought about how best to proceed. He glanced at Orchid, who remained in her catatonic state.

Tapping her on the shoulder, he asked, "May I drive you and your family to the hospital? To go and check on Fort?"

Orchid looked at him with a blank stare but reached into her purse and handed over the car keys.

Winston embraced Kristy and said goodbye to his friends and family. He gave a head nod to Marcy.

"I'll take care of everything here," she said and shooed him away.

*   *   *

They entered the hospital, and Winston strode right up to the info desk. After asking about Fort, he was given directions to the ER section. Winston started navigating the Chan family to the other side of the building, but Orchid held back.

She wiped a tear away from her eye and said, "I need to make the arrangements for Ming."

"Okay, we'll be at the ER. You can ask the staff for directions," Winston said.

She waved him away, and he took the others over to the emergency section.

The room was crowded, and Winston saw people nursing various ailments: broken bones, hacking coughs, flushed faces. Some tried to watch a centralized TV screen blaring out the latest news. Others flipped through tattered magazines. Most, though, waited with resigned expressions on their faces.

Tal shuffled over to Winston and said, "I'll ask someone in charge about Fort. Why don't you settle the others?"

Tal rubbed his aching back and attempted to straighten his posture before heading over to the intake desk. Meanwhile, Winston found chairs for the others in the far corner, right next to a buzzing vending machine. They all sat down, but nobody wanted to look at ratty magazines or munch on sodium-laden snacks.

Bright scuffed the linoleum floor with the sole of his black sneakers. "Some vacation," he grumbled.

The others seemed to agree, displaying morose faces. Were they disturbed about their interrupted family time? Or in shock about Ming's death? Or perhaps worried for their brother Fort?

He couldn't tell, and he needed them to open up. What safe topic could Winston start with? "So . . . what else did you see around San Jose?" he asked.

Viv took the bait and spoke first. "You're kidding, right?" She pulled out a pack of Bubblicious and popped a bright pink cube into her mouth.

Sandy stood up and did a tree pose. "What my adorable sis is trying to say is we drove straight here."

"No side trips?" Winston scratched his head. Most folks traveled to see the big city first, with its urban thrills plus touristy Fisherman's Wharf. And the rich chocolates at Ghirardelli's. Winston had a bit of a sweet tooth himself.

"We only had one stop to make, the Mystery Shack." Sandy stretched and sat back down.

Winston remembered Fort saying something about the vacation, that it was more of a—"Work trip, right?"

Sandy nodded. "To inspire us kids to help launch a new product line."

"Whatever." Bright sat with his arms crossed, glowering. "I vote we get out of the family business. It's doomed to collapse."

Evan stood up. "No, we just need to revamp things. Take out the cheap labor and focus on a more purposeful product, like organic food."

Viv popped her gum. "No way. We should go big and more fancy. Perfume's the ticket." She pulled out an atomizer from her purse and spritzed the air. The scent of cloying roses attacked Winston, and he covered his nose.

Sandy blinked at her sister. "We should focus on what we do best, the handbags. But make them more responsible and sustainably produced."

"Nah. Ming wanted us to *expand* the fam biz," Viv said.

Lyle zipped open his camera bag, whipped out his Nikon, and started cleaning its lens. "What about transitioning to art?"

Sandy rolled her shoulders. "You mean reprints?"

Lyle shook his head and lifted the now gleaming camera. "Originals."

"No," Evan said. "Ming wanted copies and generics. But with appeal." He used his hands to frame the air like a director capturing a scene. "What about . . . organic moss crisps? Think about it."

Viv blew a huge pink bubble. "No way you would've won the contest with that kind of idea."

This seemed to be the lead he'd been looking for. Winston's ears perked up. "There was a competition?"

Before Viv could answer, Orchid arrived in the room. She looked around a few times until Viv jumped up and down to get her mother's attention.

As Orchid approached the group, Winston got up from his chair and greeted her. "Mrs. Chan, how are you feeling?"

She gave him a hard stare. "I finished what needed to be done."

He had asked to genuinely see how she was doing, not be insensitive. "Uh, how about a snack?" Pulling a few quarters from his pocket, he pivoted toward the nearby vending machine. "Snickers? They always satisfy . . . "

She shook her head and crumpled into a nearby chair—the one he'd just abandoned to get her a snack. "I can't handle much more of this."

Heavy, plodding footsteps came toward them. Winston turned to see Tal heading their way. He appeared more hunched over than ever.

"What's wrong?" Winston asked.

"It's Fort, they couldn't help him in time. He . . . died."

CHAPTER 16

ORCHID PUT HER head in her hands and groaned. She seemed stuck to her chair in a wilted position.

Bright spluttered. "I don't understand. What do you mean?" He looked like he would lunge at Tal, but then Winston stepped between the two of them. Bright started pacing around the room instead. With his all-black attire, he looked like a shadow flitting among the chairs.

Viv stopped popping her gum and accidentally swallowed it. She made a choking noise, while Sandy patted her on the back. As soon as Viv recovered, the sisters retreated to a private corner and held hands.

Lyle laid his camera in his bag and zipped up the case.

Tal shook his head. "Fort couldn't breathe."

"He's really dead?" Evan said in a hollow tone.

Tal raked his hands through his hair, disheveling the jet-black strands. "They said we could go see him, to get closure." He looked over at Winston. "Um, family only . . . "

Winston nodded. "Go ahead. And take your time."

After the Chans left, he regretted his rash words. How long would they take? Already his cell phone showed the time as nine o'clock. He texted Kristy.

Winston: *Sorry, still at hospital.*

Kristy: *Is Fort stable?*

Winston: *He . . . didn't make it.*

Kristy: *What?! If only I had noticed sooner . . .*

Winston: *You did the best you could.*

Kristy: *The poor Chans.*

Winston: *They're getting closure now. Don't know how long it'll take . . .*

Kristy: *You have until midnight, Cinderella.*

Winston: *I'm the prince ... or Sherlock, at least. Love you, Watson!*

Winston felt a shadow fall on him. Orchid stood above him and tapped her foot. She looked composed, though tired. Her posture seemed stiff, and her stare fixed.

The rest of the Chan family stood behind her in a huddle, their eyes cast down. Some had their arms crossed over their chests in protective gestures. Viv appeared to shiver, though the room felt quite warm.

Orchid turned her attention to her family and looked each of them in the eye. "Two dead? Our family is cursed. We are burning incense tonight."

"Fire hazard," Sandy mumbled, but Orchid ignored her.

"We leave now," said the matriarch. She pointed at Winston with a jab of her finger. "You. Drive us."

Winston led them away from the ER area by crossing through the lobby. He felt almost like Mother Goose with her goslings. Except that this was the saddest fairy tale he'd ever heard of.

Before they made it to the exit, they passed by the info desk. The lady behind it stood up and waved her arms. "Mrs. Chan," she called out.

Orchid craned her neck. An expression of deep sorrow appeared on her face. "More paperwork to fill out?"

"No, nothing like that." The woman behind the desk twirled a pen in her fingers. "I just wanted to say . . . it was his choice. Remember that."

Orchid nodded once at the woman and continued walking toward the exit.

Winston puzzled over the woman's words. Why had she flagged down Orchid? And whose choice was she referring to?

He continued trying to make sense of the strange conversation as they reached the parking lot. He watched the Chan family climb into the van.

They all looked withdrawn, and he knew no one would be chatting with him during the drive. Seated in the passenger's side, Orchid reached into the glove compartment and pulled out a crinkled receipt. She wrote an address on the back of it and handed him the scrap of paper.

Winston guessed it was the address of their hotel. He punched in the directions on his phone and prepared himself for a long, silent ride.

CHAPTER 17

WINSTON DROVE BY a number of seedy neighborhoods to reach the Chans' hotel. Once he arrived, he did a double take of the name. Although a similar-looking blue and red emblem beamed down at him, the display looked off.

"Is this a Motel 6?" he asked. The number on the sign appeared almost taped on, and it lay on its side as though the *6* had decided to take a nap.

Bright spoke first. "No, that's a nine. We're staying at a Motel 9."

Winston glanced at the man's face, which looked as dour as ever. Was the guy making a joke? He turned toward Orchid, but she didn't say anything to contradict Bright. In fact, she started unbuckling her seat belt.

Tal piped up. "It was Ba's choice." He pulled out a tube of muscle rub as he spoke and slathered the stuff over his neck. "He loved knockoffs."

"Pew. Your lotion stinks," Viv said, pulling out her atomizer and spraying everything in sight with her signature rose scent.

The combination of flowers and medicinal ointment did not combine well. Winston unlocked the doors and almost tumbled out of the van in his haste to leave.

Orchid stood still in the asphalt parking lot, under a lamppost. It cast an eerie orange glow on her face. She tugged Winston's arm. "You must join us to burn the incense. The more voices making a plea, the better for Ming," she said. "Wait here while I grab the supplies."

In the meantime, Winston surveyed the motel complex. It held about ten rooms in a cramped U shape. Orchid strode over to unit number eight, inserted her key, and disappeared inside. Winston wondered whether she'd picked the room on purpose, asking for the lucky number at the front desk. After all, *eight* sounded a lot like the word for prosperity in Chinese.

Orchid soon came back with her arms laden. She chose a dark corner of the lot, away from the creepy orange of the solitary lamppost. Then she put everything out in a neat row: the packet of incense, a lighter, a large plastic cup, and a small Guanyin statue about the size of Winston's palm.

He counted the goddess of mercy's many arms. Though she was supposed to bring peace and mercy, Winston had always considered her a strange octopus-humanoid figure.

"We need dirt," Orchid said. She pointed at Tal. "You're second oldest. Go to that bush, dig under it, and fill this cup."

Tal squinted at the scraggly bush on the other side of the lot. "What will I use for a shovel?"

"Your hands," Orchid said as she pulled out joss sticks.

She handed one to everyone present. Each long red stick had a powdery yellow top. Winston rolled the incense between his hands. How had he gotten roped into this ritual? He wished he'd stayed by Kristy's side after dinner instead of going with this odd family.

Winston saw Tal in the distance whacking at the hard earth with his arms. Closer to him, Orchid began arranging the siblings in a certain order. Winston noticed an odd pattern in the way they were lined up: all of Orchid's kids first, with Bright at the rear.

Orchid then turned to Winston. "You'll be the very last petitioner."

When a tired-looking Tal returned to Orchid, she put the plastic cup he'd filled with dirt in front of the statue. Then she told Tal to stand next to Bright. The two of them brought up the back of the sibling train.

After picking up the lighter from the ground, Orchid issued directions as she lit each of their sticks: "I'll go first. Then Sandy and so on, down the line. Say your petition out loud, so the goddess can hear."

Wouldn't Guanyin be able to listen no matter what? Winston wasn't even sure what to say when it got to his turn. As he waited for the others to speak, the powerful fumes from the incense made his eyes water.

Orchid marched out first to the statue. "Oh, great Guanyin, grant my request. May Ming find rest. Let him still go on peaceful vacations in the otherworldly realm, like those we'd originally planned for our golden years." She bowed three times and positioned her burning stick in the cup of dirt.

Sandy said, "Let Ming not be a hungry ghost." Was she worried the patriarch would come back and wreak havoc on the rest of the family? Perhaps she was as superstitious as her mom.

Evan spoke next. "May there be fair wages in the beyond." Was that a dig at the substandard compensation his father had given his employees?

Lyle strode up but didn't say anything. Instead, he bowed and placed his stick next to the others. Winston wondered if Lyle's head had been in the clouds, or if he truly had nothing to say. He noticed a slight frown appear on Orchid's face.

Then Viv contributed her thoughts. "May your mercies fall on our family." Her words sounded muffled, and Winston bet she'd snuck a cube of bubble gum into her mouth.

Tal stood for a few moments staring at the statue before speaking. "Let both Ba and Fort find peace." His hands shook as he added his stick in with the rest.

This was the first time Fort had been mentioned, and Winston wondered at the significance. Was the rest of the family unable—or unwilling—to mourn for the eldest son?

Next, Bright said, "Ashes to ashes." He refused to bow but added his stick to the growing pile.

Strange. The Chan family showed very unusual reactions to grief. Some of their cries to the goddess didn't even sound that sorrowful.

Bright poked him in the shoulder. "Your turn."

Winston gulped. He walked with slow steps to the statue and tried to think of something proper to say. "May the Chan family get resolution." He did the customary bows while stifling a sneeze that threatened to explode as he breathed in the fumes. He lined his stick with the others, a bundle of eight altogether.

That "lucky" number again. Although Orchid now felt her family was cursed and had to light incense. It certainly seemed unlucky to lose two family members within the span of one day. Double *bad luck*, Winston thought. Or maybe a double *homicide*.

CHAPTER 18

O N THE MOTEL blacktop with the incense fumes spiraling up in smoky wisps, Winston saw the Chan family with new eyes. He took a deep breath. *Start with the first death and go from there. Use logic to find the killer—or killers.*

Who would want the old man dead? He knew that at least half the family didn't even refer to Ming as their father. Maybe if he could get inside their rooms somehow and investigate there, he'd find more clues.

The rooms were so close, but how could he gain access to them? A little pressure in his bladder provided him with an idea.

"I need to use the restroom," he told Orchid. "Really bad." He even did a little jig for added effect.

Orchid looked askance at him, like he was about to go right in front of her. "Come on then," she said.

He jogged with her over to room eight. As she started unlocking the door, Winston realized that Tal and Bright waited right behind them. The other Chans, however, headed next door, to room number nine. Curses! They had two units. No way would he be able to look through both without arousing suspicion.

Winston entered the motel room and caught a noseful of muscle rub. He saw belongings scattered everywhere. For a moment, Winston wondered if someone had already searched the place.

Orchid shook her head in disgust. "Boys."

Ack. They needed some serious maid service to come by. Winston tried to take a mental picture of the entire room because he knew he couldn't physically sift through all those dirty clothes and tattered suitcases.

"Bathroom's over there," Orchid said as she tried to tidy up. By this time, Tal and Bright had also entered the room, and they both made a beeline for the queen-sized bed.

"Shoes off," Orchid said. "Use the flip-flops we packed."

Then she turned her attention to Winston with a puzzled look on her face. He'd better go use the facilities before she started questioning him on the spot.

The bathroom felt cramped. It barely had enough space to house the sink, toilet, and a very slim shower stall. Would there even be anything to find in here? His eyes skimmed past toothbrushes, shavers, and floss until he saw a beige toiletry bag.

The zipper pull had a tag on it reading, "Property of Ming and Orchid Chan." He rifled through its contents, past a mishmash of items. Cosmetics seemed to take up the top half: lipsticks, blushes, and things he couldn't identify. One even looked like a miniature torture device. Made of metal, it had two looped handles with a vicious clamp at the end.

Winston heard Orchid call through the door. "You okay in there?"

"Just about done." He flushed the toilet.

Turning the faucet on full blast to cover the noise of his searching, he hunted double-time. Finally, at the very bottom of the bag, he found a half-filled pillbox. Ming's name was written on it in Sharpie. The box had the days of the week stamped on it. He opened the medication compartments and snapped a quick pic with his phone. Then he placed everything back and turned off the water.

When he opened the bathroom door, Orchid stood before him. "Was it something you ate?"

"No, I feel fine." He took a quick look around and noticed the room seemed more organized. Also, a suitcase lay open in the middle of the floor. "Are you guys packing up?"

Winston spied Tal on a bed doing shoulder rolls. Next to him, Bright lay sprawled out, snoring away. The other bed, though, seemed tucked nice and neat.

Orchid stepped into the bathroom, and her muffled voice said, "I'm going next door. Staying with the girls and swapping out Lyle."

Now, Winston could make up a good reason to check out the other room. "Mrs. Chan, I can carry your stuff over. Looks quite heavy."

"Thanks. Let me get my toiletry kit—wait, who's been through my stuff?"

She came out scowling, holding the beige bag in her hand.

CHAPTER 19

TAL FROZE IN the middle of his shoulder exercises and said, "I didn't touch your bag."

Winston knew he'd be next on Orchid's accusation list. Wasn't it suspicious how long he'd taken in the bathroom? He wanted to pull at his collar, give space to the sweat drops lodged against his neck, but that would confirm his guilt.

"Must have been Bright," Tal continued, hooking his thumb at the sleeping figure.

Orchid looked at both of her stepsons with disgust. "Don't go through my stuff with your man paws."

She placed the toiletry bag with her other belongings and zipped up the suitcase. Then she told Winston, "Go on, carry it over."

Winston picked up the suitcase, and it almost yanked his arm off. What had she packed? Rubbing his sore bicep, he pulled up the handle to roll it along.

Meanwhile, Orchid opened the adjoining interior door. It'd been unlocked. The flimsy wooden partition didn't make a sound as it swung open. Seems like the family members could cross from one side to the other with ease at any time.

Room nine was the polar opposite of its neighbor. The suitcases were placed with care in the closet, and the place seemed barely used. Even the beds looked unslept in.

Sandy and Viv perched on the edge of their tidy mattress, flipping through glossy magazines. Lyle lay across the bedspread, scrolling through the photos on his camera. He murmured to himself about focus and aperture. Only Evan seemed ready for bed with his flannel pajamas on.

"I'm moving in," Orchid announced, rubbing her hands together. "Finally, peace and quiet."

Her two daughters looked up and smiled. Winston wondered how the five of them (four adult children plus Orchid) would fit in the small room.

"Put my luggage with the others," Orchid commanded him, so Winston added the suitcase in with the rest.

Orchid hovered over Lyle as he scrutinized another photo. She tapped him on the shoulder. "You'll have to swap with me."

Lyle pressed the button once more before turning to his mother. "Don't make me go over and room with *them*."

"Bright and Tal are your brothers," Orchid said. "You young men can bond."

"Should have booked three rooms." Lyle shut off the camera and slipped it into his carrying case. "We could afford it. Ming was trying to expand the business after all."

Orchid wagged her finger at her son. "This is a family company. You know Ming's motto: *Stay together, Succeed together.* That's why we don't lock the partition."

Lyle grumbled but swung the camera bag over his shoulder.

"Besides, two rooms are cheaper than three," Orchid said. "And this space will now be a girls-only zone."

"What about Evan?" Lyle pointed at his brother, who sat cross-legged against the wall.

"He can go as well. Oh, too late." Orchid sighed.

Winston watched as Evan closed his eyes. The young man's breathing became soft and even. Could he actually sleep seated against the wall?

"Move," Orchid said again, giving Lyle a slight push.

Lyle gathered his belongings from the closet and trudged over to the adjoining door. "I'm your blood son," he said as he moved into the next room and slammed the partition shut.

Orchid turned to Winston. "Thanks for your help." She suppressed a yawn. "Have a nice rest of the night."

As Winston said goodbye, he heard thumping coming from room eight. Indistinct but unhappy voices could be heard through the thin wall.

He wondered about the division in the family and how deep it ran. After all, the original room assignments had been organized by family line: Orchid and Ming with his biological sons on one side, and Orchid's kids in the other. Had the Chan family ever melded into a happy Brady Bunch? Or was it all a facade that was starting to crumble?

CHAPTER 20

WINSTON DRUMMED HIS fingers against his chin in the parking lot. Should he go straight home? But even if he did, he knew the double deaths would bother him, making sleep impossible. He wanted to follow up on his only lead.

Pulling out his cell phone, he checked the time and texted Kristy.

Winston: *You still awake, Kristy?*

Kristy: *Yes, you back home?*

Winston: *Not yet. Think I could swing by your place? Want to show you something.*

Kristy: *Okay . . . But no peeking at the dress.*

Winston: *Won't. Cross my heart.*

Kristy: *FYI, Marcy's here.*

Winston groaned and almost changed his mind. Did he really need more big-sis time tonight? Although she was holding onto his car . . . And what if there were a murderer (or two) on the loose?

Time would be of the essence.

Be there soon, he texted.

He added a heart emoji, grinning at the phone like an idiot. She couldn't see his head-over-heels face, but maybe she'd feel his love over the pixels.

Winston called for an Uber. Ten minutes away. He started heading to the front of the Motel 9 so the driver might spot him better. While walking, he heard a car start up from behind him.

However, instead of passing him, the car seemed to follow Winston. Who was this jerk of a driver? Maybe it was a crazed teenager. Instead of cruising the streets, the youth nowadays tried to play chicken with hard-working citizens.

The car behind him wasn't focused on lurking behind like a silent threat. Winston heard the vehicle rev.

He sprinted toward any kind of protection. Maybe that line of bushes on the side would work.

Minutes later, he felt the heat of an engine near his back. He dove for cover in the row of plants.

The front quarter panel of the car still managed to nudge him. How many points was a hit-and-run worth in this insane game?

From the corner of his eye, he saw another vehicle pause near Motel 9's entrance. Winston scrambled out of the bush. He jumped up and down, waving his arms to attract the newcomer's attention. Any kind of help would be welcome.

The crazy driver of the van, a mere shadow in the seat with the vehicle's headlights off, stopped pursuing him. Soon, the car dashed toward the exit and sped out of sight.

The second vehicle eased toward Winston. Checking his app, Winston realized the license plate matched that of his scheduled ride. His Uber driver had shown up and saved him.

Winston glanced to where the road rager had gone. "Could you wait here a minute while I check something out?" he asked the driver.

"No way, man. Do you know this neighborhood? Bet I'm the only driver willing to even come this way."

Sighing, Winston got into the Uber. His hands trembled. "Did you get a good look at the other driver?"

His Uber savior shook his head. "Too dark. Couldn't even tell if it was a man or a woman."

"I wonder if I should report what happened." But Winston didn't really want to get a teen into trouble with the law.

"Well, if you do change your mind, I did notice one thing. The vehicle's color. That was one dirty-looking gray van."

"Are you sure?" Winston asked.

"Yeah." The driver clucked his tongue. "But what people do for kicks around here."

Winston couldn't stop shaking. A van? Could it have been the Chans' vehicle? Something he'd driven only hours before?

It made sense. He *had* been snooping. And he must have made one of the Chans very angry to get such a nasty warning.

What had he gotten himself into? He'd nearly died right before his wedding. What if they went after Kristy next? He'd have to make sure he was one step ahead of the killer.

CHAPTER 21

WINSTON GOT TO Kristy's place safe and sound. He saw his Accord parked in the driveway. "Good old Grayskull," he whispered, giving the He-Man-nicknamed automobile a gentle pat on the trunk before ringing the doorbell.

Kristy welcomed him in with a loving hug. "How's my hero?"

"Tired . . . and glad to be alive."

"What do you mean?" In the foyer, she held Winston at arm's length and examined him. "Are you hurt?"

"No, I jumped out of the way of danger," he said even as Kristy shook her head over the scratches on his legs from jumping into the bushes. They stung, but he wouldn't admit it.

He explained to her about how a crazy driver had tried to mow him down. Inserting some humor, he claimed he'd superheroed his way out by flying into the shrubbery.

After he finished his story, he heard a giant pop from farther inside the apartment. He flung his arm across Kristy to protect her.

Then he understood the noise. He noticed Marcy on the couch blowing up balloons—and sometimes bursting them.

The whole living room was covered in purple and white balloons. In fact, Winston couldn't even spot the carpet underneath all of the air-filled latex spheres.

"What exactly are you doing?" he asked Marcy.

She took in a huge inhale and filled up a white balloon. "Duh. Recreating your arch, Sherlock."

Ah, the curve of balloons that had graced the entryway to the wedding. "Where's the helium?" he asked.

"All I could find at this hour was . . . " She pointed to the bags of latex balloons balancing on the couch arm.

Marcy was going to blow all those up by herself? "Wow, that's a lot of work. Thanks, sis," he said, settling onto the couch.

Kristy came over with a first aid kit. She adjusted the cushions around Winston and said, "Rest." She dabbed his wounds with antibiotic ointment before bandaging them up. "Let me grab you a Coke."

When she left, Marcy said, "I overheard you talking. What's this about you almost getting run over?"

"An unidentified driver back at the Chans' motel." He grabbed an uninflated balloon from an open bag.

Marcy's eyes narrowed as she considered her brother. "Were you snooping around again?"

He held his hands up. The balloon hung loose between his fingers. "Investigating is the more accurate term."

"But didn't the old patriarch have a heart attack?"

Kristy returned with his drink right as Winston answered, "Yes . . . but Fort also died in the hospital."

"He did?" Marcy gasped. Guess she hadn't heard the news because his sister let go out of the balloon she was blowing up. *Whoosh.* It rocketed out of her hand.

"Again, I wish I'd noticed his symptoms sooner at the restaurant," Kristy said. Her face had gone pale, and she started tilting the glass in her hand, so Winston placed it on the nearby coffee table.

He hugged Kristy and murmured in her ear.

"Two deaths in the same family." Marcy took an uninflated balloon and twisted it in her hands. "What an unlikely coincidence."

"My thoughts exactly," Winston said.

Kristy's eyes widened at Winston. "It's too dangerous. Perhaps you shouldn't investigate anymore. Let the police handle things." She snuggled next to him on the couch and rested her head on his shoulder.

Winston blew up a purple balloon and didn't answer her. Should he quit? But someone was already onto him.

He was next on the hit list, and he didn't even know the identity of the culprit. He had to continue searching to protect himself and—he glanced at Kristy and Marcy—the women closest to his heart.

He tied the balloon and handed it to his sister. "I might've have found something interesting in their motel room that could shed light on Ming's sudden death."

Marcy abandoned the balloons and leaned forward. "What did you discover?" Winston knew she'd been a great asset during the Magnolia case, and he realized how alive she'd acted as she helped him investigate.

He pulled out his cell phone and found the picture of the weekly pillbox. "Ming's medicine."

Kristy asked for the phone. She zoomed in on the image.

"What do you see?" Winston asked.

She looked at it for a few moments. With her brow scrunched, she said, "This doesn't make much sense."

Marcy piped up. "Is something off?"

"Weird," Kristy said. "I'm familiar with this medication, and these bright red pills are duplicates of a powerful drug." She pointed at a time slot filled with pills of the same color.

Winston squinted to read the small letters on the tablets. They all bore the same name.

Looking over his shoulder, Marcy said, "Three of the exact tablets in one day? What's wrong with that?"

"These aren't common pills," Kristy said. "They're powerful prescription blood thinners meant to be taken on a precise schedule. Patients have to take one a day."

Winston scratched his head. "How come Ming has three in that plastic compartment then?"

Kristy nodded. "I think they got moved, and he ended up skipping a few doses. But without the medicine, blood clots could form—and lead to a severe heart attack."

CHAPTER 22

WHO HAD ACCESS to those dangerous red pills? Winston snapped his fingers. "It must have been Vivian. She was supposed to organize the meds last."

"The Chans' youngest daughter?" Kristy said. "She smelled like innocence."

Or a cloying rose scent masking something more sinister, Winston thought.

Kristy bit her lip, and Marcy said, "No need to concern yourself, Ms. Bride. It's off to bed. Big day tomorrow. You'll need to look fresh and rested."

Marcy led Kristy around the balloon spill on the floor. As Kristy passed him, Winston pulled his fiancée into a quick hug and whispered, "Sweet dreams, love."

"I'll try," Kristy said, "but I'm so worried about the Chan family. I wish they had some sort of resolution. It seems wrong to enjoy our celebration while they're still suffering."

Winston wanted to be the one tucking Kristy into bed. But, of course, he couldn't spy Kristy's bridal gown prior to the wedding. Bad luck. Anyway, he'd have his own chance to escort her tomorrow night . . .

Marcy soon reappeared, and her huge yawn brought him out of his daydreams. She started counting the blown-up balloons aloud.

"There's probably enough," Winston said.

Marcy scrunched her nose in disbelief.

"Time to sleep, sis. You staying the night?"

"I think I will. Let me text Gary and let him know." She whipped out her phone and punched a few keys.

Mere seconds later, a *ping* sounded. Winston caught a glimpse of a kiss emoji before Marcy tucked the phone away.

"I'll take a quick catnap," she said, stretching across the couch. "Get some energy to blow up more balloons. Better to have plenty on hand."

"Just sleep. We can hack together something in the morning," Winston said. Rummaging in the linen closet, he found a quilt and draped it over his sister.

Glad I have Marcy as a sister—instead of someone like that conniving Viv. He must have said it out loud, though, because she thanked him for his compliment in Cantonese: *do jeh.*

She snuggled under the covers and continued, "Too much sibling rivalry in that family. Like at rehearsal dinner."

"What's that, Marcy?" Then he remembered the hubbub at Sambal. The heated conversation in Cantonese. "What *were* they arguing about?"

Marcy positioned a throw pillow under her head. "Ming's very specific written will. He'd set aside some money for his wife, but none of the inheritance goes to the daughters, only the sons."

Old-school thinking. Females got less than a byte; they ended up with nothing because boys were "worth more" than girls.

But it did create a motive for Viv to take out her stepdad. "I need to find her," Winston said. "Bring her to the police before she escapes."

"You need more evidence," Marcy said, stifling a yawn. Her eyes started closing, and she murmured, "Go to bed, Winston. The Chans will be here in the morning. Takes time to figure out funeral details."

His sister conked out. Winston tucked the quilt around her. It was nice to be the responsible one for a change.

She'd had her turn, always being the reliable Wong. In fact, Marcy had organized the burial details for their parents. He had shown up to everything without any idea of the cost or the work involved.

As his sister's breathing slowed, Winston found his mind slipping a little into dreamland. Should he follow Marcy's advice? He *could* go home and crawl into his cozy bed. Surely, the Chans would still be around in the morning tying up loose ends.

He checked his watch. Just before midnight. What he wouldn't do for a soft down pillow at this hour.

But something niggled at the back of his mind. Evidence. He needed more concrete links to Viv as the killer. And the more time that went by, the fewer clues might remain.

Should he truly investigate at this late hour? Leads could reveal themselves after he had a good night's rest. Clear thinking could lead to greater insight.

Meanwhile, he knew Kristy might be tossing and turning with concern. Maybe he couldn't provide her with complete peace of mind tonight, but he could solve the case before their wedding.

Winston wandered over to the kitchen faucet. He splashed cold water on his face. Drying himself with a nearby dish towel, he rubbed hard at his cheeks to wake himself up.

One more stop tonight before he called it quits. He needed to go back to the exact scene of Ming's death.

CHAPTER 23

WHEN WINSTON DROVE over to Alex's place, he noticed the lights were off in the main house. Oh well. He didn't need to bother his friend anyway. He'd be in and out in a jiffy.

Winston moved through the clearing and wound his way to the Mystery Shack. He noticed the door didn't have a lock on it. Perhaps Alex didn't think there was anything worth stealing in there. After all, it was a crazy sculpture of a building surrounded by trees.

He went inside and tried to find a light switch. No dice. Figured. Probably no electricity or running water in the shack either. Winston wished he had a nifty tool holder like Batman's utility belt. He settled for pulling out his phone and using the flashlight function.

A strong stench of muscle rub combined with a stuffy floral rose scent pervaded the air. He decided to leave the door open. Not wanting to miss any leads, he combed every room in the shack, using circular search paths.

First, he went around the outer edge, walking the perimeter. Then he made tighter and tighter circles. He found nothing incriminating, only dirt and dust balls in every space he looked.

He ended up back in the middle of the main room, gazing at the staircase leading to nowhere. Why would anyone even want to climb those treacherous steps? But maybe Mr. Chan had wanted to get his full money's worth and see the drop-off.

Winston started ascending the staircase. The steps sure were slippery. Had Alex superwaxed them? Winston wanted to grab onto a banister, but none existed. Mincing his way up, he snailed it to the top of the staircase. At the peak, Winston gulped.

There was a pitch-black gulf before him. What would a tumble from this height feel like? He really didn't want to know.

He sidestepped along the top ledge—and felt something jab his ankle. He swung his phone's light toward the pricking sensation. A glint of gold flashed at him. It was a pin of some sort.

Winston picked up the item before scooting on his butt back down the steps. Better to examine it on the secure bottom step.

The pin was crafted in the shape of a rose with golden petals, leaves, and a stem. It had to be worth a pretty penny. And he remembered seeing the same brooch before—secured to Viv's shirt.

Tap, tap, tap. He heard footsteps approaching and quickly pocketed the jewelry. Or perhaps he could hold it aloft to defend himself? But that tiny pin would never be sharp enough to injure someone for real.

Understanding that the flashlight app might give away his location, he shut it off. But it was too late. He'd been found out.

A bright beam of light flashed straight into his eyes. He brought his arms up in what he imagined was a karate chop pose.

He'd never even taken martial arts, but maybe the attacker would be fooled.

The dark figure behind the flashlight seemed quite slim. A woman? Viv?

A narrow ladylike hand held up something that looked dangerous. It glinted in the flashlight like a dagger. But smaller. The sharpest nail file he'd ever seen.

"I'm friends with a cop," Winston said. "In fact, he's probably on his way ri—"

"Winston?" The light beam traveled up and down his body.

Hmm, the voice didn't sound like Viv. Could it be— "Carmen?"

"Yes. What are you doing on my property?"

He breathed a sigh of relief. "Investigating."

"The Mystery Shack? In the middle of the night? I thought you were a burglar."

"I'm looking into Mr. Chan's death."

Carmen put her nail file away. "Gaffey said it was an accident."

"You believe that noob? It's more complicated than the cop thinks. Mr. Chan and now Fort. Plus, I found something."

Carmen yawned. "You disturbed my sleep for this? Come on." She grabbed his arm with a pincer grip and pulled him out of the shack. "Besides, don't you have a wedding coming up?"

Winston checked his watch. Just after one in the morning. He didn't have much time before he needed to be back here, so he said goodnight to Carmen.

Knowing that he had a solid tie connecting Viv to the staircase made him feel better. Maybe he could squeeze in a little rest. Then he would confront her early in the morning and still make it in time for his wedding.

CHAPTER 24

WINSTON OVERSLEPT. After all that sleuthing, he didn't even hear his alarm clock. In fact, only the insistent ringing of his cell phone woke him up.

He untangled himself from his sheets and grabbed the phone.

His sister's voice hissed down the line. "Quick, you have to help me."

"What's wrong?" Winston's insides twisted as he wondered if Marcy was in trouble. Did the car break down? Was her marriage having problems again?

"These balloons," she said. "They're so hard to tie down."

Winston let out his breath. "I'll come by soon."

"You better. You're pushing the time as it is." She clicked off.

He checked the clock display. An hour before his wedding! He threw on some non-smelly clothes he found crumpled on the floor.

Did he have time to go confront Viv? No, he couldn't be late to his own wedding. Maybe he should make her come to him. She'd want her expensive brooch back, especially since none of the Chan girls would inherit anything from Ming.

After Googling the number, he called the motel. The line rang several times before a sleepy voice picked up.

"Motel 9." A yawn. "What can I do for you?"

"Can you connect me to room nine?"

"Sorry, there's only this one phone here in the lobby."

Winston thought for a second. Had the Chans left already? "Is there still a van in the lot?"

After some muffled noises, the clerk said, "Yeah. Sorta gray in color."

"That's it." Winston checked the clock again and started grabbing everything he needed for his big day, especially his tux in the travel garment bag. "Okay, take down this message."

"For room nine?"

"Yes, for Vivian." Winston walked over to his garage. He stashed everything inside the car trunk. "Say: I found something that belongs to you in the Mystery Shack. But hurry, the wedding starts in an hour."

The clerk yawned again, and Winston experienced static on the line. Was the bad reception on his side or over at the motel?

"Got it," the clerk finally said.

"You sure?"

"Found item, shack, wedding." The clerk hung up.

Winston wondered if the right message would be relayed, but he had no time to dwell on it. As it was, he would need to speed through all the yellow lights he encountered on his way to the wedding venue in order to help his sister.

*   *   *

Beyond Alex's mansion, at the edge of the clearing, Winston found Marcy and Gary wrestling with a spool of floral wire and balloons.

His sister flashed him a look of relief. "Thank goodness you're here." She thrust a pair of wire cutters at him.

Winston looked at the nearby wedding arch, which was only half-filled with purple and white balloons.

She stretched out her fingers. "It'll be great having a fresh pair of hands."

Her husband stood on a stepladder reaching for the peak of the arch and tying on balloons. "Marcy's been tying these into patterned color clusters all morning long," Gary said. "Great to have you on board, Winston."

Winston and Marcy soon developed a system for the task at hand. He held the balloons onto the arch while Marcy tied them in place using pieces of floral wire.

They were near completion when he took a moment to peer beyond the structure. Past the display of balloons, rows of white chairs were set out, ready for future guests. Alex and Carmen must have woken up early to organize the seating.

Speakers were set up near the gazebo, too. Winston and Kristy had selected their song list with care. A classy selection. The bridesmaids would walk down to Pachelbel's *Canon in D*, and Kristy would swoop in on the "Wedding March."

As if he'd summoned her with his thoughts, his bride soon appeared. Her hair had been done up in elegant swirls, and the makeup she wore accentuated her beautiful cheekbones and full lips. She wore a button-down shirt and drank a celery-colored smoothie through a straw.

Kristy's eyes twinkled as she pecked his cheek. "We'll be husband and wife soon enough."

"I know." Winston gazed at her shimmering eyes and fumbled his balloon.

"Sorry, but I need to steal your sister and get ready," Kristy said. She pointed at his *Space Invaders* T-shirt. "You will be wearing something more formal to get married in, right?"

"Yes, I stashed it in the main house. I'll change"—Winston glanced at the few remaining balloons—"after I finish this arch."

"Jazzman and Anastasia should be dropping by to prep, too." She gave him a quick squeeze on his arm. "I can't wait to see you decked out."

Winston thought about the tuxedo he'd left hanging in the downstairs marble-filled bathroom of Alex's huge house. Winston had gone all out—black and white formal. He'd even purchased silver cuff links in the shape of a deerstalker hat.

How Sherlock could figure situations out . . . Winston admired the fictional character's smarts. "I wish I had wrapped up this case before the wedding."

Kristy pursed her lips. The natural sheen on them made them look very kissable. "I know you have a theory, but Viv feels innocent to me."

"Actually, I found her rose pin on the staircase. The one Ming fell off."

Kristy used her straw to swirl the thick smoothie. "Could it be a coincidence?"

"How about the fact that she was the last Chan to touch the meds?"

"Was she really?" A shadow passed across her face, and she stopped stirring. "Remember the medicine cabinet at Sweet Breeze?"

He knew what she was thinking. For a brief period, Winston had suspected sweet Kristy of being involved in murder because she'd had access to dangerous medicine during his first big case. "But who else could it . . ."

The adjoining room in the motel. Any one of the family members might have snuck in and moved the pills. He frowned. Was he back at square one?

From his peripheral vision, Winston saw Marcy place one more cluster of balloons on the arch and dust her hands off. She went to Kristy's side. "Time to get your gown on."

Kristy smiled and gave Winston a tender hug.

Winston waved to the two women as they headed back to Alex's house. He wondered how Kristy could look even more gorgeous than she had the other day, when she'd worn that slim-cut emerald sheath. His heart thumped faster.

Turning back to the balloons, he concentrated on them for five more minutes. Then he put the last balloon in place and said, "Thanks for your help, Gary."

His brother-in-law stepped off the ladder and slapped Winston on the back. "Marriage. Boy, you're in for a wild ride." Then he folded the stepladder and headed toward the house.

CHAPTER 25

WHILE WINSTON WATCHED Gary leave the clearing and return to the house, a familiar voice greeted him. He turned around to find Jazzman behind him. The elderly gentleman wheeled a long rectangular case.

Jazzman grinned at Winston. Dressed in an elegant velvet waistcoat, the pianist could've been mistaken for the man of the hour. And Jazzman was, of a sort. He'd be playing a key song during the recessional: "Chances Are."

Jazzman shook Winston's hand with gusto. "Huge congrats are in order."

"Thanks. And we definitely appreciate you playing *our* song."

"Of course. But could you help an old man out?" He gestured to the bag he'd been pulling.

"Is that, like, a keyboard suitcase?"

Jazzman nodded and said, "I'm not as strong as I used to be. Don't want to hurt anything at my age."

Winston flexed his biceps. "You're in luck. I've been working out to better fit in my tux." He grabbed the case and started wheeling it over to the gazebo. Even rolling the keyboard along strained his back a little. How had Jazzman carried it?

"Thanks, Winston. Over there"—Jazzman pointed to the area with the sound system. A huge speaker sat on the grass with wires sticking out of it.

The two of them unzipped the bag and unloaded the equipment. They set up the stand and placed the keyboard on it.

Jazzman stretched his fingers and reached inside his vest pocket, pulling out a tiny resealable plastic bag with pills. He popped two tablets into his mouth.

The medicine reminded Winston of Ming's tampered pill box. "You remember meeting the Chan family yesterday?"

Jazzman put away the tiny bag. "Sure. They crashed the rehearsal and then the dinner. I talked to one of the sons, an artist fellow."

"Lyle? The one with a giant camera?" Winston indicated the size of the Nikon by framing his hands.

"Yes. He showed me some great snaps."

That's it, Winston thought. Photographic proof. "Did he have any photos of his dad at the Mystery Shack?"

"Of course. Ming looked like he wanted to peer into every cranny of that weird place. Lyle even took one of his dad climbing stairs to nowhere. A motion shot, though. Kinda blurry."

"Was he alone in the picture?" Winston held his breath. Might Lyle have photographed a significant shot? Perhaps the critical moment right before Ming's fall?

Jazzman dusted off his vest as he thought. "Somebody else was there. One of the brothers, the lad wearing all black."

Bright. It had to be. "Were they standing next to each other?"

"Real close. The son seemed to be gripping his father's arm."

Maybe Bright had been planning his father's death for a while. That would explain the clothes meant for a funeral. And he'd finally pushed the old man off the stairs. Because messing with the pills hadn't been enough.

While Winston formulated this theory in his head, Jazzman ran his fingers down the length of the keyboard. The pianist was probably itching to play.

Jazzman looked at the wires trailing the keyboard and frowned. "How do you connect this to the amp again?"

Winston bent over to find the connector to the speaker. He and Jazzman were still peering at the sound equipment in bewilderment when they heard someone approaching.

"I can take care of that, gentlemen," Carmen said. She was dressed in an elaborate crystal-embedded ballgown, which hugged her every curve, and carried a large satchel.

"Stand at the keys, Jazzman," she said. "And you, Winston, pretend to be the audience. Go and sit in the front row."

They moved to the requested positions. Near the sound system, Winston watched Carmen pull something out of her bag and fiddle with the wires. She turned her back to him and blocked his view with her massive gown.

Jazzman poised his fingers over the keys. He pressed down on the keyboard, but nothing played. Had the sound system gone haywire? Somehow got corrupted? But then operatic music poured out of the speaker.

Instead of the romantic ballad of "Chances Are," Winston was subjected to very high-pitched singing. "What is that?" he said, placing his fingers in his ears.

"I think that's from the opera *Carmen*," Jazzman said, a confused look on his face.

Why would a sound track be playing instead of his preplanned wedding music? Carmen turned around and winked at Winston. She twirled in her ballgown, showing off her dance moves.

The woman always enjoyed being the center of attention. But today she couldn't be. Because Kristy was the bride, the star of the show. Was she feeling bitter because of it?

Winston groaned. Carmen must have hidden a music player in her bag. Along with other things, like deadly nail files, as he'd witnessed last night. The tool was so sharp it could do some serious damage . . .

He swiveled his head toward the balloon arch. Then he turned back to Carmen, who stood before him with a huge grin on her face.

He got up and almost knocked over his chair in the process. "You were the one who popped the balloons at the rehearsal."

"That's right," she said, not a flicker of apology on her face.

He gripped her shoulders and shook her a little, making her giant purse fall. Its contents spilled. A very familiar black box toppled out. "You took my wedding bands?!"

He snatched up the precious rings. "I don't understand. Why?"

"A little payback for what you did to me." She smirked and went over to the sound system and turned off the music.

What was she going on about? He and Carmen had never been an item. Then he had a literal flash of inspiration.

A radiant light glowed around him. He *hadn't* pursued a relationship with her, and that's why she felt spite. "Is this all because I picked Kristy over you?"

"*I* ditch the guys," Carmen said. She tossed her hair. "Not the other way around."

"Sorry." Winston didn't know what else to say. "We really weren't meant for each other."

"Obviously." Carmen made a sweeping motion with her hands, encompassing her amazing mansion and its beautiful grounds. "This is what I deserve. Riches and more. And I did it by myself through publishing a bestselling memoir."

Another brilliant flash. Was Carmen now experiencing a physical illumination as well?

Her eyes narrowed at something behind Winston. "I thought you hired a professional photographer."

Winston turned around to find Lyle pointing his camera straight at him.

CHAPTER 26

WINSTON SHIELDED HIS eyes from the camera's flash and asked, "What are you doing here?"

Lyle stopped taking pictures and hung the camera over his shoulder. "We got your message. Didn't you invite us to your wedding? I caught a Lyft earlier than the rest to take some before shots."

"Wait, I did what?" Hadn't he left a message incriminating Viv?

Lyle took out a cloth and started cleaning the camera lens. "You told Viv you saw something in the shack. And to meet you for your wedding."

Winston thought back to his static-filled phone message and the sleepy clerk. He'd told the messenger about the pin and then said, _The wedding starts in an hour._

He did a face palm. He'd wanted Viv to rush and make it _before_ the big event, not to show up for it.

Lyle continued, "Everyone else is getting ready, but they'll be here shortly."

Winston took a deep breath in and out. Well, now that Lyle was here, what info could he get out of the photographer? Winston eyed the man's camera. "Do you still have pics of the Mystery Shack?"

Lyle nodded. "Didn't have a chance to upload them yet." He pulled up a picture of the front of the shack and started explaining the lighting he'd used.

Winston interrupted him. "Jazzman said you had a few with Ming on the staircase."

"Righto." Lyle scrolled through the shots, passing by a number of staircase photos. It seemed like the entire Chan family had climbed those steps. He stopped at the pictures featuring his stepdad.

One had Ming at the bottom of the steps, pointing to the top. Another had him midway. The next featured Ming—and Bright—on the stairs.

The picture appeared blurry. Bright seemed to have a hand on his dad's arm, but the details remained fuzzy. Bright's body was positioned behind Ming's on a lower step.

"What's happening here?" Winston asked Lyle, pointing at the screen.

"Bright went up the stairs with Ming. Wanted to hold onto the old man because the steps were so slippery. But Ming flung his arm away."

Was the grip not malicious then? "So Bright was holding his arm because—"

"He wanted to help. But Ming was stubborn, longed to get to the very top by himself. Which he did—right before he tumbled."

Winston patted Lyle's arm as the photographer blinked back a few tears. "Sorry."

Lyle gulped and said, "Think I'll take some pics over there." He pointed to a location across the green space, opposite from where Winston stood.

Looked like Lyle needed time to process things. Engrossed in his quick retreat, Winston jumped when somebody tapped him on the shoulder from behind.

Anastasia had snuck up on him. A large bag with ribbons spilling over the top lay near her feet. "I'm here to decorate the overly plain chairs."

She enveloped Winston in a warm hug, her layers of lilac silk swishing over his arms like waves of water.

"Need a hand?"

She huffed to herself. "Yes. Pete always runs late. Can you fill in until he gets here?"

Winston nodded, and Anastasia pulled out some lacy ribbon.

"We'll place the fabric down the aisle on both sides," she said.

They unspooled the ribbon and got busy making a fancy barrier. Anastasia also tied big tulle bows at various intervals. "So"—she pointed to Lyle—"is the Chan family crashing the wedding, too?"

Winston tangled his fingers in the gauzy fabric and choked out his next words. "I accidentally invited them. Actually, I had meant for Viv to come alone early to corner her."

"Rose girl?" Anastasia wrinkled her nose. Too much perfume for even the self-proclaimed Russian royalty to bear? "You suspect her?"

He finally removed the ribbon from his fingers and straightened it out. "She was in charge of Ming's pills before he died."

Anastasia took her forefinger, decorated with five gold rings, and tapped at her chin. "That does look suspicious."

He pulled out another spool from the bag and handed it over. "But what I don't understand is she's a girl, so there's a lack of motive. None of the Chan daughters will get any of Ming's inheritance under his old-school thinking."

"Unless she won the contest," Anastasia said while pinning a bow. They had finished one side and moved to the row opposite.

"What contest?" Winston asked, even as he remembered the Chans mentioning a competition happening during their work retreat.

Anastasia selected another spool of ribbon and gave the end to Winston. "Everyone was to present their ideas to Ming on the best knockoff product to create next. If he picked their suggestion, the person who won would get to lead the company."

Winston dropped the ribbon and scrambled to retrieve it. He dusted off the dirt. "So Fort wasn't really next in line?"

"Not by default."

"Did somebody get picked as the winner?"

Anastasia shook her head as she flattened out the ribbon. "Fort said no. Heard his loud voice gloating about it at the table during your rehearsal dinner."

They tied the ribbon down, and Anastasia placed bows along the stretch of the material. Although he stayed on task, Winston's mind reeled. Fort would've stayed in power, but with him gone, the next in line would be—

"Doesn't matter," said a man's voice.

Winston turned around to find Pete walking toward them.

"Sorry, I'm late," Pete said to Anastasia.

She put her hands on her hips while he attempted to fluff a few already prepped bows. "We're about done now."

Winston could tell she was going to launch into full-scale scolding, so he jumped in. "Pete, why would you say it doesn't matter?"

"Don't you know? Maybe you couldn't hear from your side of the table near Kristy, but I suffered next to those rehearsal dinner crashers. Everyone grumbled about it at the table. How the business was losing money. How the wife wanted to start their golden years but couldn't."

Winston swallowed hard. "And now Orchid will never get to go on those vacations."

Pete scoffed. "I don't feel sorry for that snatcher."

"What did you call her?" Winston stopped Pete from messing further with the bows.

"Orchid's a thief. I saw her steal at the restaurant. Chopsticks, forks, even something porcelain. Slipped them into a giant Ziploc."

"Was the ceramic object white?" Winston chewed on his lip. "Did it look like a mini bowl?"

"Yes, it even had traces of sauce still in it."

Winston could picture the array of delicious grilled skewers . . . and its accompanying circular container of deadly peanut sauce. Had Orchid murdered Fort? Because she sure seemed to have hidden the evidence.

But why would she murder him? Maybe it because of her stepson's gloating, the disrespect he showed for his sick father in the hospital?

A trembling seized Winston, but he soon realized it was Pete shaking him.

"Hey, Winston," Pete said. "You'd better get ready. Can't want to miss your own wedding."

Winston checked the time and sprinted to the main house.

CHAPTER 27

WINSTON RAN INTO the main house and almost crashed into Alex.

"Whoa, don't break anything," Alex said, gesturing to the exquisite-looking ceramic pieces distributed around his home. The main house was more of a museum than a living space, with its bells, whistles, and gongs. Modern art and fancy sculptures lurked around every corner.

"I'm running out of time," Winston said, sprinting toward the bathroom.

"No worries. The officiant's not even here yet."

"He isn't?" Winston shook his head and grimaced.

He entered the bathroom, finding it done up in an elegant theme of black and white. The polished floor looked like a giant chessboard. Two obsidian vessel bowls lurked over a swirled marble, chocolate-and-vanilla-scented countertop. And this was only the guest bathroom.

The wedding tux hung on the hook where he'd left it. All pressed, it glowed an unworldly white. It was a replica of Tuxedo Mario's in *Super Mario Odyssey*—but obviously much cooler.

Before he had a chance to put it on, a knock sounded at the door. Probably Alex. Winston opened it. "Did the officiant finally show up?"

"Huh?" Orchid Chan stood before him with a giant potted flower in her hands.

"Oh, I thought you were someone else."

Orchid pushed her way in, then closed the door behind her.

He gulped. What she was planning on doing? She had killed Fort for his rudeness. And Ming for what—his unwillingness to retire?

Winston backed up against the bathroom counter, and Orchid stepped even closer to him.

"This plant is my namesake," she said. "I want to thank you."

He eyed the ceramic pot the flower was in. It seemed heavy enough to crack a skull. How ironic to be beaned by a flower with the killer's same name.

"Thank me?" he whispered. For stumbling onto her wicked ways?

"You were a witness to my family's suffering." She lifted the pot up, and Winston flinched.

She edged closer . . . and placed it on the marble top next to him. Could it be some kind of subtle threat?

Winston scrambled to think of a way to make sure she thought he was on her side. "I just want true resolution for you. Peace."

She nodded and reached into her purse. Did she have a vicious nail file in there like Carmen? Or something deadlier? She yanked out . . . her phone. "Have to text the kids. They're in the Mystery Shack. Don't want them worrying. Now I'm the only parent they have."

As she sent the message, Winston recoiled. "But *you* did it."

"What are you talking about?" She peered at him, confused. Her phone dangled in her hand.

"You made Ming, er, go away." He remembered what the woman at the help desk had said at the hospital. She'd been sorry that Orchid had—

"Yes, I did pull the plug." Orchid's lips twisted. "His wishes . . ."

Winston tried towering over her. "How could you kill Ming? Aren't your marriage vows for better or for worse?" He himself would repeat those very lines soon.

"My husband fell," Orchid said, her eyes locked onto Winston. "The stairs were too slippery."

Winston leaned in. "And what about his pills? Moved so he *forgot* to take his much-needed blood thinner."

She stared at him, not blinking.

"You knew," he said.

Orchid started crying. Fat tears ran down her face. She didn't bother wiping them away.

He cocked his head and reconsidered her weeping figure. Had it been cold-hearted murder on her part? "Maybe you didn't want Ming to die, just get injured? Hurt enough to push him toward retirement."

Orchid wiped her eyes with her sleeve. He wondered if the tears would trickle down into her phone and crash its system. "No, the missing pills were . . . a mistake."

"Really? And what about the ramekin?"

She gave him a blank look.

"The little container of peanut sauce you slipped into a Ziploc? Evidence of you causing Fort's death."

Orchid shook her head several times. "I know she didn't mean to. It was a prank. And why should she get in trouble for that? Plus, I thought Fort would get better . . ."

"She?" He didn't think Orchid was speaking about herself in the third person. She could have only meant one person. "Viv did it?"

Orchid's shoulders slumped. "All a mistake. The sauce, she probably meant it as a joke. Like when she swapped the sugar with salt for his coffee."

"You saw your daughter dump in the peanut sauce?"

Orchid shivered. "No, I found the ram-a-thingy left with a stack of dirty dishes. It had to be her, right? So I took away the container."

Had it been Viv? She'd been sitting across from Fort. With the wide rectangular tables at Sambal, she would've needed to lunge across the wooden surface to slip in the peanut sauce. Winston said, "Maybe Viv wasn't to blame . . ."

Orchid continued speaking as if she hadn't heard Winston. "And the pills. Viv was responsible for those, but Google docs are so complex. Maybe she misread the column."

While she babbled on, Winston thought, Was the case really that complicated? He'd already established that Viv had nothing to gain. And even if Orchid had offed her husband, it wouldn't do to kill the successor, too. That would just make more work for her.

Occam's Razor. It was like he'd told Gaffey. The simplest solution worked the best. Who would stand to gain if those two died?

Orchid kept talking. "Why can't the medication list be on paper? Everyone always adds to the Google doc, changes stuff. It messes everything up—"

Winston gripped her arm. He had a hunch about the killer's identity, and this would confirm it. Pointing to Orchid's phone, he said, "Can you access that Google doc for me?"

She pulled it up, and Winston saw the list of medications for the previous week. In black and white, the blood thinner had been moved over to the end of the week. It'd been recopied repeatedly. And the document had tracked the user who'd changed the medication distribution.

Winston showed the person's name to Orchid, and she blanched. "But that says—"

The door burst open.

CHAPTER 28

TAL STOOD IN the restroom's doorway, his frame more upright than usual. Where was his usual muscle soreness that required a perpetual tube of smelly ointment?

Tal's eyes widened at the sight of Orchid. "Ah, the wicked stepmother, always overworking me until my body feels like it's broken. Well, all the better. Two for the price of one." After Tal marched in, he slammed the door shut and locked it.

"Why are you trapping us inside?" Orchid asked. She looked back and forth between Winston and Tal as if waiting for an explanation.

Winston pointed at Tal. "Your stepson, he's responsible for Ming's death. Didn't you read the spreadsheet?"

"That doesn't make any sense." Orchid rubbed her forehead and peered at Tal. "You're not ambitious. You always complain about the business."

Tal sneered at his stepmother. "This was my golden opportunity to stop the work abuse, to change things."

Winston could feel Tal's anger at Orchid and tried to shift the focus from her. "Why mess with the pills?" he asked Tal. "You could've won the competition and took control of the company fair and square."

Tal shook his head. "That would take too long. Ba didn't want to retire. And besides, Fort was always his favorite, so big and strong. The contest would've been rigged."

Winston could see how Tal might feel overshadowed by his older brother. Although Tal seemed quite the leader now.

Winston tried to reason with him. "Why don't you let Orchid go? She's old—"

Orchid shot Winston a dirty look, but he didn't care. He'd play the age card if he needed to. Besides, if Tal freed Orchid, she could alert the authorities.

"I can't release her," Tal said. "She knows too much and will tell on me. Besides, she's the reason we were pushed to work so hard in the first place. When Ba remarried, he gave us a ton more to do—because he had to support his new wife."

As Tal rifled through his murse, Winston tried to calm him down. "Don't do anything rash. I'm sure you can explain everything away to the police. After all, you were under a lot of stress."

Winston saw Tal pull out a familiar bottle. The baijiu he'd ordered at Sambal. Was he going to break it over Winston's head? Had Winston unwittingly paid for his own instrument of death?

Tal gestured with huge hand motions. The contents of the full bottle sloshed around. "You couldn't leave things alone, could you? Even after I gave you a warning with the van—"

"It was you who tried to drive into me?" Winston backed up against the counter. The edge of the sink dug into his hip.

"Who else? But you didn't take the hint. Kept on investigating." Tal growled out the next words. "Even left a message with the motel that you'd found something at the Mystery Shack. I thought I'd been so careful, too. What was it?"

Winston gulped. "It was . . . nothing, unimportant."

"Yeah, right." Tal twisted off the bottle cap. "Was it the muscle rub? Too much on the staircase?"

Aha. Tal's greasy ointment. That had made the stairs super slippery.

"The pills weren't enough for you to mess with . . . You had to ensure your dad fell," Winston said.

"I couldn't rely on his weak heart. Needed to up the stakes, so I made sure to grease the steps right before Ba climbed them. I pretended I was putting on my muscle rub ointment but added some to the stairs when the rest of the family wasn't looking."

That explained the lingering sharp odor in the Mystery Shack. "And how did you get rid of Fort? There were so many witnesses at the restaurant."

Tal pulled out his handkerchief and stuffed it into the mouth of the bottle. "Ha. Lots of people eating, chatting, fighting. It was super easy to slip peanut sauce into Fort's dessert."

Orchid sat down in the corner of the bathroom and started rocking. "You killed Ming. And then Fort. To take over the family business."

"Now you get it, dear stepmother." From his murse, Tal retrieved a book of matches.

Orchid stopped rocking and looked at Tal's hands. "What are you going to do with those?"

But Winston knew exactly why Tal had alcohol, cloth, and matches. And it wasn't any kind of cocktail Winston wanted to taste.

It's now or never, Winston thought. He had to find something in the bathroom to help him. Too bad old Mrs. Chan looked useless curled in the corner.

But she surprised him. As Tal lit his match, Orchid let out a blood-curdling scream. Shocked, Tal dropped his match onto the checkered floor, where it sputtered out.

Meanwhile, Winston found a weapon. He launched at Tal with the potted flower in his hands. Aiming for the base of Tal's head, he swung hard. A resounding thud. Then Tal crumpled to the ground.

Orchid screamed again, a piercing shriek that wouldn't let up. It was so loud he missed the pounding at the door. He only knew others had come to check on them when the door splintered open.

CHAPTER 29

ALEX CAME RUSHING through the broken door, wielding an axe. "What happened? I heard screaming." His head swiveled, looking around the room.

Winston knew the scene would appear odd. He himself held up the potted orchid like a shield. Orchid had stopped shrieking, and her mouth now hung wide open. Tal lay on the floor, unconscious, a broken bottle in his hand.

"Tal tried to attack us," Winston said. "But I got him good." He patted the flower pot with affection.

"Looks like it." Alex lowered his axe and stepped over to Orchid. "Are you all right, ma'am?"

Orchid closed her mouth and nodded.

A commotion sounded from the hallway. Winston heard loud clomping footsteps before Gaffey burst into the bathroom—with the officiant in tow.

Gaffey flashed his badge while the celebrant cowered in a corner. The cop's eyes narrowed at Winston. "What trouble have you stirred up now?"

"I was defending myself," Winston said, pushing the flowers in front of Gaffey's face.

The cop sneezed. He looked over at Tal's unconscious body and back to the plant in Winston's hands. "You used *that* as a weapon?"

"There's not much else in here," Winston said, placing the pot back on the bathroom counter.

Gaffey put his forefinger and thumb up to his forehead and squeezed. "And exactly why would Tal be attacking you?"

"I solved the case. He murdered his dad and Fort." Winston tried to strut, but it wasn't as meaningful in his *Space Invaders* shirt.

"Those are very strong accusations. Do you have any proof?"

Orchid straightened up and said, "I heard Tal confess. He tried to kill me, too."

Winston pointed to the broken bottle. "If the Molotov cocktail isn't enough to show you his killer nature, maybe you should check out the Google doc for Ming's medications. Tal changed up the pills."

Orchid's brow furrowed as she added, "And he greased the steps in the Mystery Shack with muscle rub. Maybe you can check for fingerprints." She patted her purse. "Plus, I have the peanut sauce container he used to poison Fort with as more evidence."

Gaffey's eyes goggled with all the information. He pulled out a notepad and started jotting everything down.

The doorbell rang then, loud and strident. A barrage of voices and footsteps headed their way. The entire Chan clan soon craned their necks around the bathroom door.

Viv squeezed inside and threw her arms around Orchid. "Mom, are you okay?"

The two seemed super close. No wonder Orchid had tried to cover for her baby girl. Winston was glad he'd kept the old lady safe and unscorched.

The other Chans tried to budge in but got stuck in the narrow doorway. They murmured at seeing Tal's prostrate body.

"What happened to Tal?" Lyle asked, even as he lifted his camera above his siblings' heads and snapped photos.

"This is official police business." Gaffey lifted his badge high in the air. "No bystanders."

The Chans' voices grew more animated.

"I'll tell you everything," Orchid said to them as she motioned her family away. The other siblings disappeared from the doorway, but Viv remained.

She stopped before Winston and said, "Excuse me, but I think you found something in the shack? Could it be . . . ?""

Winston reached into his pocket and pulled out the rose brooch. "All yours," he said.

"Thank you. It's a family heirloom." She pinned it on. "Now I'm ready for your wedding."

The wedding! Winston hardly noticed Viv excusing herself as he turned his attention to the officiant in the corner. "And why are you so late?"

Pointing to Gaffey, the celebrant said, "He pulled me over and started questioning me."

"You stopped my officiant?" Winston asked Gaffey.

The cop shrugged. "Doing my job. Kristy told me about that van following you. And this man was driving a gray-colored car."

"A sedan," the celebrant said, scratching his bald head.

A suspicion surfaced in Winston's mind. He stood eye to eye with Gaffey. "Was this really about helping me—or hindering my wedding?"

A flush bloomed on Gaffey's cheeks. "Well, I had to try, didn't I? Delay the inevitable somehow."

"You are definitely not invited to the ceremony," Winston said as he grabbed the tux from the back of the door. "But in the meantime, you can arrest Tal."

Alex piped up. "What a mess," he said as he surveyed the room. "I'll have to pay the maid double."

"Oh, the problems of the rich," Winston said. Which reminded him . . .

"Here are the rings," he told Alex. "Courtesy of your girlfriend who happened to 'find them' in her purse."

Alex gave him a puzzled look. "Huh. Guess I didn't look there. Well, you can change upstairs," he said to Winston. "I'll let the crowd know we'll be starting soon."

Winston began heading out, but Gaffey called him back. "Congrats," the cop said.

"Yeah, I'm glad to put this case to rest."

Gaffey pulled at his earlobe. "I meant you deserve your detective title . . . *and the girl.*"

Winston nodded at Gaffey's compliments. "Don't worry. Your time will come." Then he hung his tux over his arm and left to get ready for what would be an insanely great wedding.

CHAPTER 30

STANDING NEAR THE gazebo, Winston thought he didn't look half bad in his rented tux with the Sherlock cufflinks. He fidgeted with them as he watched the bridesmaids glide down the runner lying on the vibrant green grass.

He hadn't known what he was missing until Kristy walked into his life. Or rather, he stumbled into hers after somebody had fat-fingered his ad and introduced a typo in it. His new "seniors' sleuth" title gave him a case at the local retirement home where she had been working.

An indignant yowl brought him out of his reverie. Blueberry was led down the aisle on a leash by the ring bearer, Kristy's genius toddler nephew, and her sister-in-law. The little boy kept yanking on the line, and Blueberry protested every move forward.

Blueberry didn't appreciate his role as flower cat, as it required a silk bag stuffed with rose petals attached to his collar. But as he jerked forward, the cat shook his body and deposited the petals everywhere. At the end of their stroll, the boy's mom picked up both the toddler and the cat and deposited them in the front row.

Finally, the strains of the "Wedding March" started, and Winston took a giant gulp. Kristy soon came into view and looked amazing in her formal gown. Swaths of sheer fabric enveloped her, enough to satisfy even Anastasia's taste. A long train trailed behind Kristy, and she wore a glittering tiara on her head. A delicate veil attached to the headpiece fell behind her chestnut locks.

The rest of the ceremony proceeded with Winston in a daze. He even had to be prompted by the celebrant to take the ring and slip it onto Kristy's finger. He just remembered staring into her warm brown eyes, which felt like home, and disappearing from the rest of the world.

Only after the sweetness of their kiss and the pronouncement of "Mr. and Mrs. Wong" did Winston finally notice the gathered crowd. While Jazzman played "Chances Are," friends and family clapped and beamed as he and Kristy made their way down the aisle.

Then he and his bride (!) stood in the back to receive the guests as they exited. Everyone wished them well and gave them compliments on the wedding.

The Chan family was the last to congratulate them.

Standing before Kristy, Orchid wiped away a tear. "You look lovely."

"Thank you." Kristy planted a kiss on the older woman's cheek.

"Your joy today reminded me of my own wedding with Ming." She turned to Winston. "Thanks for figuring out what really happened to my husband . . . and to Fort."

He looked over the rest of the Chan family. Their faces appeared mixed with emotion as they clustered around Kristy. Though they gave her hugs and warm wishes, he knew it was a bittersweet day for them. How would the family function without Ming and the two oldest sons?

"I hope you can all move on and go forward from here," he said to Orchid.

She clasped his hand with both of hers. "Yes. I'm going to burn more incense to Guanyin for greater mercies in the afterlife. And plead to the god of war to wreak havoc on Tal."

"Oh. Er, may Ming and Fort rest in peace. And justice be done through the judicial system," Winston said.

Orchid motioned for Viv to step forward. "We have a gift for you, Winston."

The youngest Chan daughter carried a giant bag in her arms: a neon-orange briefcase done up with sequined tiger stripes. "For you," Viv said, running her fingers across the smooth part of the bag's surface. "The finest in pleather."

"Uh," Winston said.

Kristy saw him floundering and gave the Chan family a sweet smile. She adjusted Winston's hands around the briefcase. "This could be useful for holding your detective gear."

Winston averted his gaze from the garish orange color and mumbled, "Yeah, thanks. Very thoughtful."

After he shook each of their hands, the Chan family filed out of the clearing. Then he turned to his bride.

"Business is officially done," Winston said. "Time to party."

They had booked a fancy ten-course banquet at a nearby Chinese restaurant. And after eating, they'd go straight to the airport. Winston couldn't wait to start their honeymoon.

*   *   *

After the delicious banquet reception, Winston and Kristy changed from their fine attire and went to the airport. Their flight was delayed, but they spent their time chatting about the wedding banquet. In the middle of a detailed description of the succulent roast duck, Marcy and Gary appeared at their boarding gate.

His sister hugged them. "Congratulations again." Then she plopped her luggage next to their seats. Gary stood behind Marcy, his hand resting on the handle of his rolling bag.

"What are you doing here?" Winston asked. Had she finagled a special gate pass to say goodbye? Or maybe she was waiting for a show of gratitude for her help. She *had* booked the honeymoon trip to Tahiti, he remembered. "Thanks again for making the arrangements."

"Yes, it'll be so fun to explore Tahiti together." She looked over at her husband and held his hand. "Our hut isn't too far from yours, Winston."

Kristy's eyelids fluttered. "Really?"

Winston groaned. "Marcy, it's a *honeymoon*."

"Gotcha!" Marcy laughed and started gathering her luggage. "You should have seen the look on your face."

Gary shook his head but smiled. "She wanted to play a joke on you. Saw your flight was delayed and decided to sneak up on you."

Marcy pointed down the corridor. "Our gate's that way. Direct flight to London."

"Let's go home," Gary said, placing his hand on Marcy's shoulder.

They left Winston and Kristy with a cheerful wave, Marcy still letting out a few chuckles.

The gate attendant informed them that their flight was now boarding. Winston and Kristy walked over to the scanner and passed over their tickets. Two boarding passes. He loved seeing *Kristy* intertwined with *Wong*. The pair of them together for life.

Kristy tugged on his sleeve. "Come along, Winston. You don't want to miss our honeymoon."

"Yes, Mrs. Wong." He linked arms with Kristy as they moved onto their next adventure.

ACKNOWLEDGEMENTS

Thank you for reading *Wedding Woes*. If you enjoyed this book, please leave a kind review online.

Make sure to check out my other writing at www.jenniferjchow.com/books. And you can sign up for my author newsletter for additional updates at http://eepurl.com/Y52yj.

Again, I'm grateful to Linda G. Hatton for her eagle eyes and honed editing skills. Much love to a supportive creative community, particularly my writing group, Sisters in Crime, and Crime Writers of Color.

Thank you goes out to my family for inspiration and encouragement. Also, hugs and kisses to my groom, Steve, who has supported my writing from the very beginning.

Made in the USA
Monee, IL
20 July 2021